GD

The Gallows at Gila Bend

A vacancy has appeared in the riverside settlement of Gila Bend, Arizona. When the incumbent marshal, Bill Owen, is killed by a drunk, the English aristocrat Born Gallant steps in to fill the void. Little does he know that his spell as this town's badge-bearer will be far more eventful than he predicted. . . .

He won't have to handle the danger alone, though. With the help of some old companions, he must bring peace to a town under the shadow of murder, a bank robbery and corruption.

By the same author

The Killing of Jericho Slade
The Bloody Trail to Redemption
El Dorado Sojourn

Writing as Will Keen
McClain
The Outlaws of Salty's Notch

Writing as Jim Lawless
The Gamblers of Wasteland

Writing as Matt Laidlaw
Mohawk Showdown

The Gallows at Gila Bend

Paxton Johns

A Black Horse Western

ROBERT HALE

© Paxton Johns 2020
First published in Great Britain 2020

ISBN 978-0-7198-3071-6

The Crowood Press
The Stable Block
Crowood Lane
Ramsbury
Marlborough
Wiltshire SN8 2HR

www.bhwesterns.com

Robert Hale is an imprint
of The Crowood Press

Typeset by
Derek Doyle & Associates, Shaw Heath
Printed and bound in Great Britain by
4Bind Ltd, Stevenage, SG1 2XT

PART ONE

PROLOGUE

They hit the family's remote home at three in the morning, long outer coats folded into their saddlebags so that when they dismounted they were shadowy figures blending into the Stygian gloom, unrelieved by stars or moonlight. In a small corral behind the house a horse whickered a greeting. One of the men cursed softly at the sound as they ground-hitched their horses and trod soundlessly up the grassed sides of the gravel path. Then, once across the small gallery that creaked under their weight, they used the double blast from a shotgun to shatter the lock of the front door, destroying the quiet of the night.

From that moment they moved with speed.

The stairs were taken in long strides. Knowing that the childless married couple would prefer a front bedroom, they kicked that door open and entered the perfumed warmth with an explosion of sound.

The curtains were open. There was enough faint light from the window for them to see a man scrambling from the bed, falling awkwardly to his knees as his legs became entangled in the folds of his nightshirt. One of his hands slammed on to the small bedside table for support, rocking the unlit brass oil lamp. The other fumbled for the pistol lying on the pages of an open book.

Behind him, a grey-haired woman was lying on her back in the bed, clutching sheet and blankets to her throat, her eyes wide and staring.

The tall intruder with the shotgun used it to club the man to the floor. Then, when he rolled groaning on to his back, he rammed the weapon's muzzles into the soft flesh under the dazed man's chin. The violence and the fall rocked the table. The lamp fell, lay on its side. The stink of spilled coal oil began rising from the carpet.

The tall man's stocky companion was already around the bed. He dragged the woman out from under the covers. In her fear she was moaning. Terror made her legs too weak to bear her weight, and she sagged against her attacker. He held her from behind, his arm encircling her body in its thin nightdress, holding her under her arms, her breasts.

The first words were spoken by the man with the shotgun.

'Does your wife know the combination?'

'Yes.'

'Where are the keys to the door?'

'Here, in. . . .'

'Get them.'

The shotgun was eased away from the man's throat. He sat up with difficulty, turned, and from that awkward position again stretched a hand towards the bedside table.

'Don't do it, not unless you're tired of living.'

'You asked for the keys, they're in here.'

He slid open the small drawer. The keys, several of them, were on a big steel ring. They jangled as he handed the ring to his attacker. And now, with that man's attention temporarily distracted, he did make a desperate lunge for the six-gun.

The shotgun swung high and down and knocked him flat. He lay still, not unconscious but too dazed to react, to pose a threat. At the crack of the steel barrels hitting his skull his wife, still held by the second man, began to weep.

'Shut up,' the man holding her said. 'Put on a gown. You're going for a ride.'

His face against the oil-soaked carpet, the downed man said hoarsely, 'No, for God's sake, leave her here with me. You've got the keys. I'll give you the combination, you can take what you want, just leave us alone. . . .'

'You'd lie. We'd get there, the keys would open the doors but the combination would be random numbers tumbling out of your fear. She goes with me. If her memory fails, or the combination fails to work, she dies – and then I come for you. My friend with the shotgun will make sure you're still here when I get back – and

7

you'd better hope your wife is with me, alive and well.'

'All right, if that's the way it has to be, but let my wife get dressed. . . .'

'No.'

The woman was shaking so badly it took her almost a minute to find and don her dressing gown. Barefoot, she preceded her captor down the stairs and out of the house. He forced her to mount his companion's horse, awkward in her nightclothes, paying no attention when gown and nightdress rode high to expose naked knees and thighs.

There was still no moon.

There were no neighbours near enough to hear them passing in the night.

With the sobbing woman leading the way and always aware of the six-gun that would send a bullet into her back if she tried to flee, they rode away from the house in its small secluded clearing, and on into the Arizona riverside town of Gila Bend.

CHAPTER ONE

'This is where you'll spend most of your time.'

The Gila Bend town councillor, Ed Logan, stepped to one side. A tall, spare man wearing a dark serge suit, he had a look in his eyes that was both intelligent and speculative. Waiting for a response. Interested in what it might be, but not showing concern.

Born Gallant walked past him, into the office of the stone-built jail. A deputy was standing back in the shadows. The impression Gallant got was of another tall shape, mostly dark, the glitter of a badge at chest height, weapon some way below that, gunbelt, brass shells with the dull gleam of Inca gold.

'What I'm expecting is at most a very short time,' Gallant said to Logan, 'if you do your job. Get someone in here, local, capable. An English tenderfoot's a bit out of place, wouldn't you say?'

He stopped by the desk, turned. Logan was still in the doorway. He was blocking most of the light, which wasn't much anyway: the street's oil lamps fighting the night dark, some kind of weak illumination reaching

9

them from the saloon a couple of buildings away, a brighter window across the street, the warmer glow from a sun long gone behind the western hills.

'Tenderfoot doesn't match your growing reputation, Gallant – but, yes, of course we will. But with the incumbent marshal gunned down by that. . . .' Logan jerked a thumb towards the cells '. . .that drink-soaked skunk in there, we needed a . . . a stopgap.' He smiled an apology in the gloom, at once sensing the insult in his words.

'Marshal Bill Owen. Famous – or maybe that should be infamous, from what I heard across the saloon bar. Certainly something of a legend. But wouldn't his right-hand man have been the logical choice?' Gallant gestured at the silent deputy.

'Normally, yes, Dan would have stepped in, filled the breach.'

'Stopped the gap?'

'Yes.' A grimace. 'But he and his wife are expecting their first child. I, we . . . we need a man with his mind wholly on the job.'

'Of making sure a killer stays locked up.'

'For the next day or so. No more than that. He'll hang, for sure, but there'll be a council meeting tomorrow morning. A new marshal will be sworn in as soon as a decision is reached. As for tonight, I hear you've checked into Ma English's place, the Bend's one hotel.'

'No.' Gallant shook his head. 'Well, all right, I have booked a room, gave the old dear a glimpse of my countenance – but tonight I stay here. If I'm to look

10

the part, even for a short spell, I need to soak up some atmosphere, because as town marshal I'll be wearing a badge. For me, that'll be a first. As for . . . Dan. . . ?' He looked at the deputy.

'Dan Makin,' the tall man said huskily, the first words he'd spoken.

'Right, so, you go home, Dan. I've got newspapers to read, a heap of Wanted dodgers, a chair to sit on, a desk where I'll rest my feet.'

'Or there's an empty cell.'

'Thanks, but no thanks,' Gallant grinned. And then he waved a hand, already taking on responsibility, slipping on the mantle of authority that came naturally to a man born into a family of titled landowners. 'Go home, make sure your wife's comfortable, give her my best wishes.'

Logan shut the door when the deputy had gone. Gallant found the hanging oil lamp, from the iron stove lit a splinter of kindling and got yellow light to force the shadows into retreat. For the first time he took a good look around.

He'd seen better offices, in better towns. And many worse of both, most on a hot sub-continent where bearded men wore white robes and carried long-barrelled weapons called Jezails. The desk was a scarred roll-top, up against the side wall beneath a fading calendar, and some kind of framed certificate with an illegible date. The ancient swivel chair creaked when he gave it a spin. There were filing cabinets here and there, and a shiny padlock secured a locked steel cupboard where he knew the town's lawmen would store rifles, shotgun, maybe the good coffee that would be a magnet for the light-fingered.

That last reminded him he hadn't eaten since breakfast. He took the coffee pot from the stove's top, weighed it, lifted it for Logan to see, got a nod. Tin cups were on a dusty shelf. He poured coffee into two of them, handed one to the councillor, shifted papers and hitched himself on to a corner of the desk.

'Unless you intend starving him to death,' Gallant said, 'that gent snoring away out back will need feeding.'

'Sal's bringing food over. Sally Adair. She runs the café, stays open late. I told her two meals.'

'His name?'

'Foster. He says.'

'Not local?'

'A drifter, a saddle-tramp. That was the first impression.'

'But?'

'Too confident. He was drunk when he murdered Bill Owen. Sober, he got a look in his eyes. Like he's laughing at us.'

'So maybe,' Gallant said, 'he wasn't all that drunk when he executed an exceptional lawman. Maybe he had his reasons.'

'Or his orders? A deliberate killing? If that's so, and it wasn't a personal grudge that kid in there was settling, then why, and what follows?'

'Well, you heard what I said: all I'm here for is to make sure the killer stays behind bars.'

Logan sipped his coffee. Walked a few paces, did

some more thinking, shook his head.

'Yes, and that's the way it'll pan out, because there's surely nobody damn fool enough to risk a jail break to free that scum . . . The kid's a range tramp. Like rolling tumbleweed, he drifted into town on a ragged piebald, drank himself stupid, killed the best damn marshal we ever had, and now he's behind bars. In a couple of days or so he'll drift right out again, by way of a gallows and a strong rope.'

'Did Owen leave a family?'

Logan flashed a sharp look at Gallant.

'What are you getting at?'

Gallant said nothing. Eased his position on the desk's sharp corner. Waited.

'They're south Texans, so what I know I got from my drinking time with Bill,' Logan said. 'His father's Will Owen, never been out of Texas, an old man in his seventies, early eighties – Bill wasn't sure. He had three sons. Bill was the oldest of them. He never married, but was well loved. His going will hit his brothers hard.'

Gallant nodded. 'Well, doesn't that suggest extreme caution's required?'

'Caution is always required when a cell is occupied, which is why you're here. But the surviving sons are miles away. Young Texans who put maybe a thousand miles between them and their hometown, but have never come close to Gila Bend. In my opinion they'll be satisfied when Bill's killer's dangling from the end of a rope.'

He put his coffee down on the desk unfinished, offered his hand – changed his mind and brought a badge out of his pocket. Gallant stood, pinned on the badge, then grasped the proffered hand. The councillor's palm was warm, dry, the handshake full of confidence.

'A fool would have had no original thoughts,' Logan said. 'By raising those possibilities you've given me all the proof I need that we've chosen the right man. As a stopgap,' he added, grinning.

'A stranger rode into Gila Bend,' Gallant mused. 'Black clothes white with dust, hair like long dry straw under his flat black hat, blue eyes bloodshot from the desert heat. He slid in an ungainly manner from a lathered roan, saw the animal cared for and stabled, then downed a cold glass of ale in the saloon. Damn fine feeling. Bucks a chap up no end, but that didn't last long. Out of the blue he was press ganged, ended up in here wearin' a tin badge. Means something, gives him a slice of power to back up his Colt Peacemaker. But why? You say chosen, but was it a choice made out of desperation? Badge offered here and there, no takers, then, glory be, a nobody rides in with brains addled by the desert sun?'

'You were recognized.'

'Really? Gila Bend's a long way from Kansas City.'

'But what you did there was in newspapers, coast to coast. You rescued a pretty young lawyer from an outlaw gang, were involved in the downfall of a corrupt politician.'

'The young lawyer brought him down. In a court of law.'

'But you already had a reputation. Journalists

14

weren't slow to list your exploits. Successes.'

Gallant snorted. 'I'm an English aristocrat who got lucky, with the help of friends who held my hand.'

'Maybe,' Logan said, smiling. 'If so, I hope your luck holds. You spend a couple of days with your feet up on that desk, and leave town with some cash in your money belt. Not,' he added with some embarrassment, 'that you need it.'

And then he was gone.

Gallant listened to the bang of the door, the sound of boots on the street's dusty surface, fading fast. He looked out of the window. Across the street, the bright light he'd noticed shone from the steamed-up window of the café. Once again he thought of his hunger. Of the man out back in a cage, Foster, waiting for what could be his last meal before death.

But what form, Gallant wondered, would that death take? How would Bill Owen's killer die?

A stupid question. He was due to hang. Even now, behind the jail, a carpenter was working on the construction of a gallows. But along with his gnawing hunger, suddenly Gallant felt the first stirrings of a totally unexpected unease.

CHAPTER TWO

Pacing the dusty office, waiting with some loss of patience for the evening meal to arrive, Gallant thought with amusement of his earlier, brash pronouncement. He had spoken of pinning on a badge he was not accustomed to, and in truth, the situation he found himself in was alien to anything he had ever known.

Born into a family of landed English gentry, after a university education he had gone on to serve as an officer in the British Army, fought tribesmen in Afghanistan, been on the fringes when Indian sepoys mutinied, and returned home only when his father died. But not to take over the vast estate he had inherited. Instead, he had chivalrously and with relief dumped the whole rich rural pile on his sister's fair head and crossed the Atlantic in search of adventure. He'd begun by getting involved with the Pinkerton Detective Agency, in the course of an investigation had dealt out death in Salvation Creek, and there had met the beautiful trainee lawyer, Melody Lake. Shortly after that he had strolled into his Kansas City hotel room to find himself staring into the muzzle of a '73 Winchester held by journalist Stick McCrae – the name 'Stick' given to him after the composing stick used in newspapers' letterpress printing processes.

And so it had begun, and continued, Stick and Melody always showing up to hold Gallant's hand when his dealings with outlaws got sticky, and violent. As they frequently did, Gallant thought, smiling.

But his recent fight to the death with Chet Eagan at the end of the corrupt politician affair had been a solo effort, and had signified the end of his extended stay in Kansas City. The vast flat plains of the north had never held much attraction for a man used to the lush, rolling hills of England and the harsh mountains of the Hindu Kush. Gallant had bid farewell to Melody Lake and Stick McCrae (nothing unusual in that), and headed south.

There had been hints during those farewells that Melody herself would soon be on the move. Bringing down a corrupt politician was a feather in her lawyerly cap, but other feathers had been ruffled. Rumblings of discontent in the City's legal quarter had threatened to burst out of control, and Melody had been of the opinion that before that happened she should break camp and depart.

Not knowing what had been decided – Stick, he supposed, had returned to his job in Dodge City – Gallant had pushed west through northern Texas, south through New Mexico, and crossed the border into Arizona. Had damn near made it to Yuma and the final border crossing that would take him into California where the blue Pacific coast beckoned. But he'd been caught cold in Gila Bend – another smile – and dammit, here he was, a blue-blooded English aristocrat, don't you know, playing at jailer in a hot, lazy town on the Gila river. . . .

The door banging open broke into Gallant's thoughts. A woman, Sal from the café, had used her ample backside to force her way in. Tall and buxom, wrapped in a full-length soiled white apron, damp grey hair pinned back, she carried two tin plates which she placed on the desk. Steaming, laden with ham and eggs, fried potatoes, bread soaking up the grease. When she stepped away, Gallant was looking into a pair of twinkling blue eyes.

'The poison,' Sal said, 'is in the plate on the left. Don't get 'em mixed up.'

The jail-house was a low structure built on one level, the street frontage narrow. Gallant found heavy iron keys on a hook. The three cells were reached through a door at the back of the office. They were adjoining cages with frontages and dividing walls of iron bars, on the left of a narrow passage. The passage's wall had high windows overlooking a side alley. During the day, those windows would provide light for the cells. Now, the only illumination came weakly from the oil lamp in the office, from a hanging lamp in the passage, the wick turned down low.

Owen's killer was the only prisoner, a huddled shape covered by a thin blanket on a rickety wooden bunk in

18

the first cell.

Gallant was unaccustomed to law enforcement, but too wise to take chances. He opened the cell door, slid the plate on to the dirt floor, locked up and returned to the office. No words were spoken. The earlier snoring had ceased. On the bed, Foster hadn't stirred.

The food, when Gallant sat down at the desk to eat, was excellent, the coffee kept hot on the stove and now extra strong. All done, the savoury grease mopped up with the hunk of bread provided, suddenly Gallant was at a loose end. The papers he'd moved earlier so that he could plant a haunch on the desk turned out to be fliers from Yuma, Phoenix and Gila Bend businesses advertising goods at knock-down prices. Faded Wanted dodgers showed the indistinct, sketched faces of outlaws, many probably long dead. Newspapers in an untidy stack were dry and crisp, brown with age. Their content, Gallant discovered, was now only of vague historical interest.

Keys on a hook alongside those for the cells opened the steel locker's brass padlock. Gleaming rifles, Winchesters, an old Henry, and a scarred American Arms 12-gauge sawn-off shotgun. No coffee. Well, the brew was drinkable, but not special enough to be kept under lock and key. He locked the cupboard, wandered to the window, then opened the front door and stepped out into the cooling night air. Took a deep breath, smelt sage, coal oil, the inevitable dust. A Mexican rode by on a mule, big sombrero colourful in faded reds and yellows, those drooping moustaches many of them wear. He glanced across at Gallant with liquid eyes made darker by the night, touched a hand to the sombrero's fringed brim. Gallant nodded in return, listened to a burst of laughter from the saloon and felt a sudden longing for cold beer.

He went back into the office.

And . . . and now what?

Was this what he'd meant by soaking up the atmosphere?

He grimaced, thought of the hotel room he'd booked and could now be resting in if he hadn't sent deputy Dan home to his pregnant wife. But the alternative was there in front of him, so. . . .

He sat down in the creaking swivel chair, lay back, tipped his hat, used an outstretched foot to shift the empty tin plate along the desk then planted both feet up there in its place. The very act made him realize how tired he was. It had been a long day, most of it taken up by the long ride in another day of searing heat. He'd had no time to wash, to freshen up. Conscious of the stink of his own sweat, he closed his eyes. The oil lamp hanging over the desk was still lit, but not bright enough to disturb a weary man. He smiled thinly. Yawned. Let the night quiet close in.

How long did he sleep? He had no idea. All he did know was that he was snapped back to full, shocked wakefulness by the hard pressure of a ring of cold steel grinding into the nape of his neck.

CHAPTER THREE

The six-gun was cocked noisily. It was a heavy weapon. The thumb's action took effort, opposing force driving the cold steel harder against the base of Gallant's skull.

'Stand up.'

'To be knocked down again?'

'If you make a wrong move.'

'Is there a right one?'

But now Gallant was talking for the sake of it because suddenly it seemed likely that Foster hadn't been working alone, and this might or might not be his partner, but only a fool would make any kind of a move against a man holding a cocked six-gun to his head.

But standing, as he'd been asked, involved bending his legs to lift his feet off the desk. Bending the legs meant that at some time they had to be straightened. One way was by dropping them and standing up. But there was an old proverb, something about different ways of skinning a cat. . . .

Gallant lifted his feet off the desk, bent his knees, then rammed both feet as hard as he could against the

21

desk's edge. The swivel chair was catapulted backwards on loose casters and it hit the standing gunman hard. There was a whoosh of breath forcefully expelled. The cocked six-gun was dragged up and away from Gallant's neck. The front sight raked his scalp. But there was no gunshot. Somehow the gunman managed to keep the hammer from falling, to prevent the firing pin hitting the cartridge.

Instantly, that told Gallant the man was desperate not to make a noise that would announce his presence to the sleeping town.

But if the man wanted quiet, the six-gun was an empty threat.

There was a strangled curse. Almost knocked off his feet by the shock of Gallant's move the man was fighting to regain his balance. Gallant stamped both feet on to the dirt floor, spun the chair. He let its momentum throw him out of it, the way a rodeo rider is tossed from the bucking Brahma bull. The gunman tripped over his own feet as Gallant shot from the chair. Another expletive turned the air blue as the man tumbled backwards. Gallant followed, sprawled all over him, arms spread, desperate to get his hands on the six-gun.

But a second man came out of nowhere. There was a flash of steel, caught in the light from the overhead oil lamp. A vicious blow to Gallant's skull, igniting another dazzling flash, a red flare, a flame somewhere behind his eyes. Hand outstretched, clawing at the fallen man's wrist, his gun hand, the last thing he saw was that flash of red light. Then he was falling into

22

darkness. A noise like rushing water might have been his senses departing, never to return.

Gallant had been unconscious many times, sometimes for minutes, and once for a whole day, when his mount broke a foreleg and dumped him on rocks in a narrow arroyo. This time it was nothing – a shadow cast by a thin cloud crossing the moon, a man closing his eyes and opening them almost at once to find he's missed nothing of importance.

The gunman Gallant tackled must have bucked him off when his colleague delivered the savage head blow. Gallant had been thrown hard against the gun locker. He recalled the sound of his head hitting the steel door, a dull bell tolling. He'd regained consciousness in a sitting position, up against that same door – now dented. Pain from the pistol-whipping knifed through his skull. A warrior's pride made him stifle an involuntary groan. He leaned forwards, rubbed his face with both hands, a man waking from a pleasant postprandial doze.

His holster was empty. They'd taken his six-gun. It was on the desk, cylinder empty, brass shells scattered. He risked feeling the back of his head. Touched a sticky spot that was as tender as a new boil.

One of the men was across the room, near the street door. He was tall, and wore a dirty white duster coat that would have covered the bed of a working girl turning to fat. It was buttoned high on his neck, the ragged hem brushing the top of his boots. His face was covered by a fading red bandanna. Knotted behind his neck, it was folded into a triangle and masked him from just below his eyes all the way to the buttoned top of his duster where the bandanna's end was tucked. His flat grey hat was pulled down at the front so that dark eyes glinted at Gallant through a narrow slit of an opening. He had a six-gun loose in his hand, and was pacing; one way, then the other. Waiting. A little nervous. Always on the side of the door well away from the only window, careful not to be seen by any drunken Gila Bend citizens weaving their way home from the saloon.

Keys jingled merrily. Footsteps, approaching. A scrawny man walked out of the passage alongside the cells and into the office. Foster, up on his feet. His rough range clothes, worn thin by use, were now badly crumpled from his time spent curled up under the thin blanket. Beneath a battered sugar-loaf sombrero his face was unshaven, lined and tanned by sun and wind. Yellow teeth were bared in what might have been a grin, a nervous tic. Behind him a second man in long duster, shorter, stocky, the same bandanna mask, a pulled-down black hat.

Twins, Gallant thought, the pair in dusters. Or maybe just brothers. Was that what this meant?

That second man held the bunch of keys high, let them ring, catch the faint light. He gestured to Gallant.

'If you can stand up, do so. You're going for a short walk.'

'Let me guess,' Gallant said, and he put a hand on the top of the gun locker and pulled himself up to stand unsteadily. 'You two, you're doing this for your brother.'

24

'Brother? What the hell are you talking about?'

Gallant smiled. 'Your grades must have been right down there on the dirt floor, don't you know – if you ever did go to school. Because even if I'm wrong, a man with his wits about him would have said yes. Grabbed hold of the opening. Dumped a whole parcel of blame on the shoulders of two law-abiding men who, maybe reluctantly, have settled for a hanging.'

'For Christ's sake, lock him up, the man's loco.'

That was the man near the door. Still nervous, but no longer pacing, the black eyes seeming to warn Gallant. He'd got a second six-gun from somewhere when Gallant wasn't watching. Foster's. Gun belt and weapon dangled from his free hand.

Ignoring him, Gallant said, 'You, Foster, have you thought this through?'

'You ever been in a cell waiting for the dawn drop, hearing a chippie hammering nails, in your ears the crack of your neck breaking? Then suddenly, you're free as a bird? Hell, what is there to think about?'

'Owen had two sons. These two here are so wrapped up their own mother wouldn't know them. Do you?'

'Does an old wolf crawling on his belly out of a cage care who left the door open? Maybe you should be praying instead of talking. You and me have changed places, you're the man in trouble.'

And now Foster was gone, the first man ushering him out into the deserted street where pale moonlight leaked through a dusty mesquite ramada, and Gallant was taking that short walk along the narrow passage with its high windows, into the vacated cell, the clang of the closing door and the key ringing in the metal lock like notes from Saint-Saëns' *dance macabre.*

He heard the second man walk away, listened to his footsteps crossing the office, the thump as the street door was closed. Gallant didn't move. Where would he go? Behind him, the door was locked. The light from the office oil lamp was just about strong enough to throw his shadow across the floor and show him the wooden cot, the thin blanket that had covered the huddled body of Foster, the scrawny nobody who had gunned down Bill Owen.

It was gone midnight, he guessed, but not by much. Hours to wait before someone – Ed Logan, Dan Makin – came banging in out of the dawn light, cheerfully hollering for the temporary marshal who'd been hired to fill a breach, stop a gap.

Well, Gallant thought, savagely throwing the stinking blanket into a corner and perching awkwardly on the edge of the cot, the gap had sprung a leak, Mary Mapes Dodge's little Dutch boy had gone to sleep. Foster was out and running. The two men who'd worked the jail break had seemed to know what they were doing, and before the town rolled out of bed, yawned and stretched in the dawn light, they had enough time to put many miles between them and the gallows at Gila Bend.

CHAPTER FOUR

'Do you need to see a doctor? His name's Olson. Maybe you should get your head looked at?'

'You think it would help? One man locked in a cell, the whole town asleep, and still I let him get away.' Gallant shrugged. 'Maybe that should have been anticipated: any army's biggest weakness lies with its sentries, they tend to fall asleep.' His smile was wry. 'That's not an excuse, by the way. There *is* no excuse.'

'I was referring to the wound, not your brain,' Ed Logan said. He seemed miles away, reflecting on what had happened. Then he looked thoughtfully at Gallant. 'The wound, it doesn't look serious.'

'I'll live.'

'Two men, you say. And your thinking, your *reasoning*, is they were Owen's sons?'

'It's possible.'

'No, it's not.'

'There's nobody out there with more reason for

wanting personal involvement in Foster's death.'

'You have a fine turn of phrase. Very English. But Owen died less than forty-eight hours ago. The elder of his brothers is a deputy marshal in Tucson. The younger boy was last heard of far north in New Mexico.'

'Well, that puts me in my place. News of their brother's death would take time to reach the deputy, might never get to the other chap. But distance is the clincher: not even the deputy in Tucson, on a fast horse, could have got here by last night.'

'Exactly. So we need to look at other possibilities.'

It had been the dark-suited Logan who strode down the passageway and let Gallant out of the cell. That had been ten minutes ago, six-fifteen, six-thirty by Gallant's reckoning, light from the distant eastern sun already painting the jail's high windows. The councillor had made no comment. Hell, what could he say? So they'd trooped through to the office, and from the swivel chair in front of the desk Gallant had told the story to a town councillor who had at first listened on his feet, then slumped into a straight-backed chair with a shake of his head.

'Other possibilities,' Gallant said now. 'Right ho, so how about it wasn't one man involved in Owen's death, it was three. Foster was the man pulled the trigger, Owen was down, but Foster then was caught. The gallows loomed. So now his pals had work to do.'

'Why would three men want Owen dead?'

'This is your town. How would I know?'

'Fair comment. And as far as I know, Owen had no

28

enemies. But if Foster was a range tramp drunk on strong whiskey, who gunned down Owen for no damn reason at all – which is what I believe – then who were those two men?'

'I don't know.'

'What if . . .' Logan hesitated, looked towards the window, back at Gallant. 'Damn it,' he said softly. 'Look, Gallant, you were all over the newspapers, praised to high heaven, the walking embodiment of one of those old-time knight fellers. . . .

'Knights errant.'

'Right. Yes. But word is you're a maverick, working for the law, but using methods that, well. . .'

'What's this leading to?'

'The possibility that those two men in duster coats don't exist. . . .'

'Jesus Christ. . . .'

'. . . and that you opened Foster's cell, walked inside, he whacked you over the head with the six-gun you'd returned to him, then locked you in the cell and walked out into the night.'

'Why?'

'Now it's my turn to say I don't know.'

'Yes, and it's best you keep your damn mouth shut, Logan. The short time in this job we spoke of is done. I'm out of here. . . .'

The street door banged open. A man held it with a stiff outstretched arm before it came back to hit him in the face. An old face, bewhiskered, sharp blue eyes beneath tangled eyebrows and a head of straggling white hair through which early sunlight filtered. In bib-and-brace overalls he was as lean as a fence pole, but more gnarled and twisted. His arrival brought with it the ripe stink of horses.

His gaze passed over Ed Logan, spotted the badge on Gallant's vest. 'Get that gallows out back chopped up for firewood,' he said. 'Your deppity's out at Boot Hill, starin' at a man been strung up from that lone pine.' He nodded at Logan. 'You'll know the one I mean. Right close to the plot where they planted Bill Owen. No names mentioned for the feller got his neck stretched, but I'd say Bill'll be resting a mite easier in his grave.'

'Don't make much sense,' Deputy Dan Makin said. 'He's in jail, certain to be hanged. Why risk a jail break so they can string him up?'

Gallant, still fuming at the councillor's blunt accusation, had ridden with Logan to the cemetery on a slope overlooking the Gila river. The old hostler had stumped back along the street to the town's stables, but he'd been right about the hanged man's identity. Makin had cut him down, left him lying under the tall tree. Even though the dead man's face was distorted by the horror of slow strangulation, he was easily recognizable to Gallant.

'Difficult to say this without sounding disrespectful,' Logan said softly, 'but this doesn't put you entirely in the clear,' he shot a look at Gallant. 'Though I will admit it makes your involvement less likely.'

'So clear your mind of nonsense,' Gallant said bluntly. 'Two men locked me in a cell, brought Foster here and hanged an already condemned man from that tree. If I was town marshal I'd be like that feller in the cheap hotel's downstairs room waiting nervously for the second boot to drop. Know what I mean? This is the start of something, Logan. Foster was freed, then hanged for a reason.'

'He was already heading for the gallows.'

'Then maybe he knew something he could use for bargaining when the rope was around his neck. Don't ask me what. Forget about me. Put your mind to figuring out what could happen next.'

'Too many possibilities to settle on one with certainty. But I do know that that gallows behind the jail wasn't built for nothing. Foster died elsewhere, but I'm damned sure there'll be more deaths, and the gallows will see some use.'

'Not necessarily. You're a councillor. You know that with good policing in a small town, crime can be controlled, deaths prevented.'

'For the time being you're still town marshal.'

'No. I told you, I'm out of here. Dan, he's more qualified, knows people, knows places. Give the badge to Dan, up his pay.'

'I told you, there will be a council meeting. Earl Sedge is head man, he'll officiate, I'll put Dan's name forward, but until then. . . .'

'Until then you've got a marshal's office but no marshal.' Gallant snorted his contempt. 'You should realize that what went on last night is not the finish, it's the start of something. And that something won't be for the good of Gila Bend, so. . . .'

He broke off.

A rider was coming fast across the rough ground above the cemetery, letting his horse pick its way. Dan Makin walked across to intercept him, reached the fence where they'd left their mounts with dropped reins, then waited, hands on hips.

The newcomer drew to a halt, dismounted, left his horse with the other three. He approached Makin, but his eyes were looking towards Gallant.

'Something going on here?'

'Nothing out of the ordinary,' Makin said easily. 'This is a cemetery, there's a dead man over there.' He shrugged, again waited. The newcomer said nothing, still looking across at Gallant. 'So,' Dan Makin said, 'you are. . . ?'

'That your town marshal over there?'

'I asked a question.'

The newcomer went to push past him, but Makin grabbed his arm. The newcomer, taller than Makin, tried to wrench free, failed, and closed with the deputy.

'Leave it,' Gallant called. 'Dan, let him come.'

The tall man, both hands gripping Makin's shirt front, hesitated, then released the deputy, followed it with a stiff-armed shove. The angry deputy stumbled backwards, but the tall man turned away and walked over to Gallant.

'I'll repeat *my* question,' he said. He waved a hand at the badge still pinned to Gallant's vest. 'You're the Gila Bend marshal?'

'As of yesterday. Temporarily. Now over.' He

unpinned the badge, tossed it underhand to Ed Logan.

'I'm getting a bad feeling. I'm here for a reason.'

'Keep talking.'

'There's a dead body over there. A severed rope hanging from that tree. Even from here, I can see the dead man's not Bill Owen.'

'It's a man called Foster. Was.'

'You were Gila Bend marshal. Temporarily. But no more. Does that mean Bill gets his job back?'

Gallant looked at the silent Logan, wondering if he'd supply the information, or act cagey.

Logan coughed, shook his head. 'Bill Owen is dead,' he said. 'That man' – he waved a hand – 'that man Foster gunned him down. We don't know why, and we don't know why two men broke him out of jail then hanged him here, in Boot Hill.'

There was a silence that dragged on. Some noise reached them from the nearby town, but not a hubbub: ordinary folk, beginning their ordinary, every-day business – the squeal of wagon wheels, the distant neighing of a horse, the faint ring of metal as a black-smith set to work – there was nothing harsh enough to disturb a cemetery's peace.

The newcomer was looking across the coarse grass to where Foster was lying on his back, face swollen, open eyes staring vacantly up at the rope that had been cut too late, through the branches of the tall tree to skies that were already white hot.

'You don't know. . . .' the newcomer echoed, his voice low but rich in sarcasm. 'Well, gents, you can rest assured that I'll make damn sure that changes.' He looked at Gallant. 'I'm here because Bill Owen sent for me. I'm Eugene Owen, Bill's kid brother.'

CHAPTER FIVE

'Why did Bill send for you?'

'He didn't say. He used the railroad's telegraph service, no details so I knew he was leaving the full telling of it until I got here. Urgent, that I do know, which suggests there was nobody he could trust here in Gila Bend. But I was in the far north of New Mexico. Urgent loses meaning when the man someone's crying out to for help can't be found for almost a month.'

'That long?' Gallant frowned. 'Wouldn't he have lost patience, sent for his other brother? A known location, closer to home and a lawman to boot?'

'Arnie? Well, I thought about that. The possible answer was that, as an El Paso deputy marshal, Arnie couldn't just up sticks and walk away for God knows how long. As a marshal himself, Bill would appreciate that. But the conclusion I came to was that the only way Bill could see out of his troubles would mean crossing a line: he could see a time fast approaching when he'd be forced to toss his badge in a drawer and take the law into his own hands.'

They'd left Ed Logan out at Boot Hill waiting for the undertaker, ridden back into town – on the way moving off the trail to let through a shiny black hearse pulled by a high-stepping chestnut mare – and left their mounts to doze at the rail in front of the saloon.

After the dazzling Arizona sunshine the long room was as cool and dim as a woodland cave. Shafts of sunlight from two high, cobwebbed windows were reflected from bottles on shelves behind the bar, from the stout barman's long, greasy black hair – and from the shiny butt of a six-gun. The Colt was worn, slung low, by a tall man at the bar's far end. His back was to the room, but he could see everything through the big, fly-blown mirror behind the shelves of bottles. One booted foot on the brass rail, he drew hard on his cigarette. The red glow touched high cheekbones, the brim of a black hat, and turned the eyes that followed Gallant's progress into the eyes of a devil.

Eugene Owen had taken the easy route to a table near the door. Gallant carried drinks over, wondering if a single night as a stop-gap marshal during which he'd been clubbed to the ground had made him over-sensitive to danger. Not so. The tingle in his backbone was a sixth sense in action. He trusted it implicitly. It was a warning that the man with the red eyes of a devil was watching him all the way.

Now, their glasses empty of beer, he pondered on Owen's last remarks. Then he nodded slowly.

'I got it from Logan that your brother was a Texas Ranger.'

'That's right.'

36

'So how long had he been the Gila Bend marshal?'

'A year, eighteen months, maybe.'

'And in that short time he became, according to Logan, the best marshal ever to wear the town's badge.'

'Bill had a reputation that rode ahead of him with pennants fluttering, announced his coming with blasts from a distant trumpet. He was a legend in the Rangers. Stayed down in the junior ranks out of choice, spent most of his time with rough colleagues quelling trouble – and I guess at times causing it – around the wild towns of south-west Texas: Laredo, Nuevo Laredo.'

'Nuevo Laredo's not Texas. It's across the Rio Grand, out of their jurisdiction if such irritatin' technicalities trouble the Rangers,' Gallant said. 'But those young men'd see that as a jolly part of the job, wouldn't they? Galloping over the bridge into Mexico to outwit the *Rurales*, cross swords with the bandits. I'm a comparative stranger in a raw, untamed land, but the way I heard it, those Ranger fellers write their own rules. Uphold the law, yes – or their version of it – but because they get judged by results they're not always law-*abiding*.'

Owen flashed a grin. 'Damn it, that could be Stick McCrae talking about you.'

'This is gettin' more interestin' by the minute. Insults tossed in my direction before I've introduced myself.'

'Born Gallant,' Owen said. 'Insult not intended. You're that tow-headed English aristocrat who gave up everything to cross an ocean and ride out as knight errant. What folks back in your home country would glorify as a modern-day Robin Hood.'

'Makes me sound uncommonly gallant, if you'll pardon the pun, but there's an implied insult in suggesting I use methods not too far removed from those of your brother's maverick Texas Rangers,' Gallant said.

'Not intended, and those methods haven't stopped your name and face from being plastered all over the front pages of newspapers across the land.'

'And now I feel like a bally mountebank,' Gallant said, 'because in that political wrangle it was Melody Lake who was prime mover from beginnin' to end. As for Stick McCrae, isn't he getting his fingers stained with ink on a newspaper many miles north of New Mexico?'

'He got out of Dodge. I first met him there, a year ago, knocked him flat on his back in the street when I was tossed bodily out of a saloon. A pattern emerging there, because it was in a saloon in Los Alamos that we got talking again. Apparently that business with the crooked Kansas City politician earned him journalistic points but made a lot of enemies. He put out feelers, got a bite from the editor of a newspaper in Yuma.'

'Glory be,' Gallant breathed. 'But if Stick's movin' south, that leaves Melody Lake all on her lonesome in that windswept Kansas wasteland.'

'In Dodge City, McCrae was never close enough to her to be of any comfort. Besides, Lake is experiencing the same animosity. She made other lawyers in the city look like cowards, or at best shirkers. Many of them have good client bases. Lake's finding it difficult to get work.'

'As she was when I left town. Even then she was restless. But did she give Stick any idea of her plans?'

Owen shook his head.

'And you?'

'Bill sent for me because there's something going on and he was worried. He ends up dead. Then his killer is found hanging from a tall tree overlooking his grave. That positioning might have some significance, might not. But the hanging can't have been done as a warning for me because Bill told nobody of his intentions.'

'But he did send the message from the telegraph office. A telegraph operator can be bribed to pass on useful information.'

'Yes, that's true, damn it.'

'You said Bill could see a time coming when he'd be forced to throw in his badge. Does that tell you anything?'

'As a lawman, here, he never put a foot wrong. Worst he had to cope with was cowboys drunk on Saturday nights, whooping it up, firing off six-guns to add to the bullet holes already drilled in dry timber walls.'

'So if trouble did come to Bill, it came sneaking up on him out of the murky shadows of his past. His past was – according to your telling – spent mostly with the Rangers in south-west Texas.'

'All the time we've been talking I've been thinking hard, but picking up bits and pieces from your comments. Outwitting the Rurales, crossing swords with bandits? That's what you said, and it's certain those incursions ruffled Mexican feathers. Those of evil *hombres*. Powerful men in a southern land of *pueblos*, poor, hard-working *paisanos*. But for a threat to follow Bill all the way north to Gila Bend it must have more behind it than some moustachioed bandit leader who got his britches burnt. We're no more than eighty miles from Mexico's northern borders, but more than ten times that from Nuevo Laredo.'

'I hate coincidence,' Gallant said, 'but I think that's what did for your brother. Trouble didn't follow him here, it found him. Two men – three, if you include the hanged man, Foster – rode into Gila Bend on some kind of lawless mission; if we're right in our thinking, they came over the border from Mexico. Minds set on a target of some kind, damned if they didn't find it here, wearing a badge, a man who in a different guise had harried them without mercy.'

'A mission, you say?'

'It's a grand name for something that could be down and dirty,' Gallant said, grinning ruefully. 'They saw your brother as a threat. But a threat to what? Any ideas?'

'Only one,' Eugene Owen said, 'and it's staring us in the face. There's nothing in Gila Bend worth the killing of a town marshal and an unexplained hanging other than all that gold and green money locked away in the bank's big safe.'

CHAPTER SIX

Later that night, standing by the window in his unlit first-floor hotel room, Born Gallant had time to reflect on what had occurred since he rode into town when, his mind set on the blue skies and endless beaches of California, he had been greeted as the saviour of Gila Bend.

Very little of what had happened would be inked in on the credit side of his character. A reputation that he always considered unjustified had seen a town marshal's badge pinned on his waistcoat by Ed Logan. Twelve hours later, that reputation was in tatters and the prisoner he had been posted to guard was hanging from a tall tree in Boot Hill.

The coming of Eugene Owen to Gila Bend had been a surprise, when it should have been expected. Hell, Bill Owen had been gunned down for no damn reason anyone could discover. A deputy marshal in Tucson had his hands tied because of his job, but a footloose drifter bent on revenge would need to do little more than saddle his horse and hit the trail. That Eugene

Owen had done, and at Boot Hill demonstrated a strong character, which boded well for the coming days. With that strong character had come a rare intelligence: their long talk in the saloon had been fruitful, even if the fruit they had plucked had yet to be identified and could well be discarded as of no use.

It was now approaching midnight. Looking down and to the left from his window, Gallant could see the small stone-built jail. Yellow lamplight spilled from the small front window. There had been a hastily convened meeting of the town council, and Dan Makin had been sworn in as town marshal. Now, Makin would be at home with his pregnant wife, and the junior deputy, whom Gallant had never met – who had become more senior with the promotion of Makin – would be sitting at the roll-top desk guarding the empty cells.

The saloon was still open for business. The lamps had been turned low. A couple of horses dozed at the hitch rack. Would one of those belong to the man in the black hat who had stared with the red eyes of a devil at Gallant's reflection? If so, what, if anything, did he have to do with the men who had clubbed Gallant to the jail's hard earth floor, then taken the prisoner to Boot Hill where his neck had been stretched?

Could any or all of this, Gallant wondered, be leading up to a bank robbery, as Eugene Owen had predicted? And if it did, to what end? To what use would the bank robbers put the loot? Was it feasible that the trouble in Gila Bend had its roots a thousand miles away in the southern border town of Nuevo Laredo, and that the stolen money would be taken

42

across the border into Mexico?

Possibly. But not necessarily to Nuevo Laredo. And if not, where, then? And why?

Questions, questions, Gallant thought wearily, looking along the street to his right were the bank was the second of the town's low-slung stone structures. And all without an answer; saloon talk had been productive, but now, juggling endless possibilities in a bare room without anyone to agree or contradict, was mind-numbing. It was getting him nowhere.

Owen had left town after his talk with Gallant. He would unroll his blankets, he'd said, in the shade of trees on the banks of the Gila River. It had been a long ride south. A hotel room would be claustrophobic for a man who had spent many nights sleeping under the stars. It could also turn out to be a chamber of death if his brother's killers came hunting.

Unlikely, Gallant thought. In his estimation, with Marshal Bill Owen out of the way those *hombres* from south of the border – if they existed – would now concentrate on the reason they had been sent to Gila Bend. And he was giving himself a mental pat on the back for his good sense – albeit still not knowing what the hell he was talking about – when the man in the black hat came out of the saloon and started across the street towards the hotel.

CHAPTER SEVEN

The hotel's entrance from the street was up a short flight of rickety steps. The front door was always unlocked, encouraging custom. From the front door, a narrow passageway with a high ceiling led past a steep flight of stairs to a scarred reception counter. On the counter there was a leather ledger, an ink bottle, a couple of pens in a rusty tin can, and a brass bell with a wooden handle. The bell could be picked up and rung to summon the hotel's owner. It had reminded Gallant of those used by town criers.

The small rectangular area behind the counter was under the stairs. If anyone was in there, they could not be seen from the front door. Hanging from a hook under the stairs, an oil lamp with a tin shade like a Chinaman's hat was kept lit, day and night. Its light touched the oak counter, leaked into the passageway, but didn't quite reach the front door.

Moving fast, Gallant padded down the stairs and was behind the reception counter before the front door opened. The overhead light turned his dishevelled hair into a shining golden cowl. His blue eyes were in deep shadow. The Colt Peacemaker was loose in his hand, hidden behind the counter.

He heard the outside steps creak. The door opened, letting in a waft of cool night air, the cry of a distant coyote. Spurs tinkled musically as the man in black stepped inside. He paused there, blocking the moon-light. Used his foot to ease the door shut behind him. Stayed there, silent, unmoving.

Use of foot, Gallant thought, meant that the man's dominant hand was occupied. In the dim light behind the counter, he smiled.

For a few moments there was nothing to be heard. It was as if both men were holding their breath. In the tense silence Gallant took a backward step. That took him further into the shadows, brought him against the wall behind the counter – the hotel's outside wall. His shirt brushed a big paper calendar, causing it to rustle.

A giveaway.

'Someone there?'

Deliberately, Gallant crooked the thumb of his right hand and cocked the Peacemaker.

'Gallant?'

'Maybe,' Gallant said. 'Or maybe it's just a poor hotel proprietor defending his property against an armed intruder.'

'You've got yourself cornered, Gallant,' the man in black said. 'Even a man with courage would have diffi-culty coming from behind that counter when the intruder controls the passageway.'

'In such a situation a man lacking courage might

fire a single shot into the ceiling to alert the new town marshal.'

'You won't do that.'

'Then it's an impasse, don't you see, old chap. Neither of us can move. We could be here all night.'

'Put your gun on the counter. I'll drop mine – you'll hear it fall.'

'Trust in the devil? I don't think so.'

'Then trust in me.'

A woman's voice rang out, clear and bell-like. It was followed by the sound of another weapon being cocked, this one clearly not a six-gun. Footsteps tripped lightly down the stairs. Above Gallant's head the boards creaked. He heard the thud of a heavy metal object hitting the passageway's board floor. When he stepped from behind the counter he saw, in the dim light, the man in black. His hands were held high, palms forwards. He was being confronted by a dark-haired young woman holding a cocked shotgun.

'This,' Gallant said, 'is getting to be embarrassin'. Seems that any time I get into any tight situation, my unworthy life hanging by a slender thread, from over the hill the cavalry comes riding up, in the shape – and there's no better word for it – of the beautiful Melody Lake.'

'Your room or mine?'

Gallant grinned at the young woman. 'The use of either one might offend the proprietor's sensibilities.'

'Ma English. She's old, broad-minded, happy to stay in her room. I told her everything was under control.'

'With you, I'd expect nothing less.'

The man in black had seen his weapon rendered useless, but was unfazed. He said, 'Why climb the stairs, disturb the old woman? That reception desk looks like it would suit a lawyer.'

'Well, well, well,' Gallant said. 'More and more people are poking their noses into other people's affairs. Disturbs a chap no end. What's your name, feller?

'Aitken.'

'And why d'you want me out of the way?'

'That's nonsense. I came here to talk. And it's Ranger Aitken. I'm a Texas Ranger, working out of Houston.'

He looked warily at Melody Lake and her shotgun, then flipped his vest open far enough to show the badge pinned to his shirt. He got no further. Suddenly Lake was on him, the shotgun's double muzzles rammed into his ribs.

'Unpin the badge,' she said softly. 'Throw it to Gallant.'

'You realize what you're doing is against the law?'

'In this town, in most towns I know, the law is the local marshal, and over the marshal there's the sheriff of the county.'

'In Texas, I'd ride rough-shod over both of 'em.'

'I'm gettin' heartily sick of hearin' all about this *macho* reputation,' Gallant said. 'Rangers carry out illegal raids for gain using the laws they're breakin' as justification. Gullible citizens see them as folk heroes, but whatever they are, whatever they're seen as, outside

Texas they're nothing.'

'That's quite a speech. . . .'

'The badge.'

After a moment's pause, Aitken unpinned the badge and tossed it to Gallant. Gallant looked at it, at the star in a silver circle, tarnished, battered. He turned it over – and looked up at Aitken. His blue eyes were mild, almost friendly.

'Where did you get this?'

'What? I'm a Ranger, we're given a badge. . . .'

'No. The State of Texas never did provide Texas Rangers with badges. So . . .'

'All right. If you must know, I ordered it from a jeweller's in Houston.'

'Yes, I've heard that way of getting 'em's standard practice. But if the badge is nothing more than a tin souvenir, you've got no way of proving you're a Ranger.'

'I am what I am, I don't need to prove anything to you.'

'Also,' Gallant went on, 'a friendly marshal I knew up in Dodge – or it might have been Abilene – told me that a lot of lawmen like to scratch their name on the back of their badges. Use the point of a knife, something like that. Driven by pride in their calling, I'd imagine, though I know that scratched name can come in useful for the identification of a dead body – especially so for a Ranger in the badlands, if demise comes as the result of Indian savagery.'

He was musing aloud, painting a vivid word picture in his listeners' minds while turning the piece of tin in his fingers. Now, when he flicked his gaze up from the badge, his blue eyes had hardened.

'Gila Bend's town marshal, Bill Owen, was shot dead. He was gunned down by a drunken kid named Foster, who was arrested before the gunsmoke cleared. The body was collected from the saloon by the undertaker, Eli Gaunt, and buried in Boot Hill. So how come you walk in here with Bill Owen's Texas Ranger badge pinned to your shirt?'

Aitken shrugged his shoulders. 'That name was on the badge when I bought it. A cheap used item, from stock the jeweller had on display in his shop window.'

'Your talk is cheap, not the badge,' Melody Lake said. 'You're looking for inspiration, but coming up with words of straw. You remind me of shyster lawyers who struggle to shoot down my cross-examination in a court of law, or a saloon bar serving that purpose. It never works for them, and it won't work here in a Gila Bend hotel lobby.'

'Turn around, Mr Aitken,' Gallant said. 'Leave your six-gun on the floor. Open the door and go down the steps. When you reach the street, turn left and make for the jail. You're about to spend a wakeful night tossing and turning in the shadow of the Gila Bend gallows.'

They'd thumped their way to the bottom of the steps, Aitken in the lead, when Gallant heard the tinkle of breaking glass. Out of the corner of his eye he caught the flash of bright light illuminating a window high above the saloon.

His reaction was instant, but still too late.

'Aitken,' he yelled, 'get down!'

His words were punctuated by the vicious crack of a rifle shot. Aitken obeyed the shouted warning, but the action was involuntary: the bullet from the rifle had taken him above the left ear and pierced his brain. Legs bereft of all strength folded under him. His body crumpled into the dust of the street.

Melody Lake had also seen the muzzle flash, and reacted.

As Gallant shouted the warning she leaped down from the high side of the steps. Taking advantage of the deep shadow they cast, she leaned back into the angle where the top step met the house and settled the butt of the double-barrelled shotgun into her shoulder. She fired a single shot, emptying one barrel. A spray of buckshot crossed the street, hissing through the night air. But even as she pulled that single trigger and felt the powerful recoil against her shoulder she was cursing softly and in a manner unbefitting a young lady. It was a shotgun, for God's sake. The scattering of soft pellets had no hope of reaching, let alone harming, the target. It was nothing more than an act of defiance, a warning to the shooter that his location had been spotted.

Gallant, down on one knee alongside Aitken with his fingertips probing the man's warm neck in a vain search for a pulse, was similarly at a disadvantage. Against a rifle, at that range, his six-gun was worse than useless. He heard the blast of the shotgun, knew at once that any lead that reached the saloon wouldn't have the power to puncture a paper bag, and abandoned the dead man. Expecting at any moment a

50

bullet to stop him in his tracks, he sprinted across the street with his shoulders hunched as if to ward off a shower of rain. With his back against the nearest store's wooden front, he wiped bloody fingers against his pants and gazed across at Lake.

'He's shot his bolt,' he called, and grinned at his choice of words. 'He's gone, down the stairs and out, on a fast horse and running for the hills.'

The shotgun's barrels glinted as Lake spread her hands. She was up on her feet, and now used the still-smoking weapon to point down the street.

The rifle shot, followed by the more powerful blast of the shotgun, had not gone unnoticed. Yellow lamp-light spilled into the street in front of the jail as the door banged open. The light was bisected by a long, shifting shadow as Dan Makin, the new marshal, came out of his office. Six-gun in hand, head turning from side to side, he walked unhurriedly but with purposeful stride towards the action. As he approached the saloon, a few late-night drinkers emerged warily, broken glass crunching under their boots. They stopped there, then backed off into the shadows as they watched the marshal walk past them without speaking, then caught sight of the dead man lying in the street.

Melody Lake walked across to join Gallant.

'Why him?' she said. 'Should have been you, or me – or both of us. But he cleared that window of glass, fired just the one shot, and it took down Aitken.'

'The man I was guarding in that jail was taken away by two men in an audacious break, then hanged by his

51

rescuers.' He shrugged his shoulders as Lake looked at him sharply. 'This looks like similar unexplainable madness, Melody, so don't ask, because I don't know.'

The rumble of wheels cut off Melody Lake's reply. As if it had been waiting around the bend for an inevitable shooting, the same hearse that Gallant had seen near Boot Hill, drawn by the same high-stepping chestnut mare, came down the centre of the street, then pulled over to come to a creaking halt alongside Aitken's dead body.

'He's got second sight,' Marshal Dan Makin said, indicating Eli Gaunt, the frock-coated, top-hatted undertaker. 'Never misses a trick. And that was some trick, waiting in one of the saloon's upstairs rooms to gun down a defenceless man. Who was he, d'you know? The dead man?'

'His name was Aitken. But the man with the rifle?' Gallant shrugged his shoulders. 'Who knows? And now there is Logan,' Gallant said, pointing. 'Either got sharp ears, or he was in a position to see what was happening. Where does he live?'

'The council offices are across the street from the jail. Logan has the floor above.'

'So his window overlooks the street, and that *includes* the jail,' Gallant said. 'No fun for you, a town marshal constantly aware of his boss looking over his shoulder.'

He watched as Ed Logan moved away from the offices, stood with hands on hips, looking from a distance at the hearse and Eli Gaunt bending over the crumpled shape. Then, with a shake of his head, the councillor crossed the street, heading for the jail.

'Is your deputy in there holding the fort?'

'Rick Lyon. He could be out on his rounds, but if he's in the office he's tough, and thick skinned enough to outface belligerent councillors trying to browbeat him. But it's you two Logan will want to talk to, and now's as good a time as any.'

Without waiting for a reaction, Makin turned on his heel to retrace his steps. As she and Gallant set off after the marshal, Melody waggled the shotgun. Her dark eyes were dancing and there was a mischievous look on her face

'I'm walking around like Calamity Jane, don't you know?'

Gallant barely managed to suppress a grin at her cheeky use of his own oft-used and deliberately silly idiom.

'Who?'

'Martha Jane Carraway. Quite a gal, apparently – and among other exploits a scout for General George Crook. I'm emulating her, swaggering up the street with loaded shotgun at the ready.'

'And talking like a dandified English toff. Well, after you sprayed the street with lead that deadly weapon's only half loaded, but still useful. We'll tag along after Dan Makin, and talk to Ed Logan. . . .'

'D'you trust him?'

'Logan? Why do you ask?'

'For some reason your words set alarm bells ringing. Tinkling faintly, anyway. My lawyer's brain, looking for double meanings, hidden depths. You said Logan either has sharp ears, or was in a position to see what was happening. So up pops a supposition: what if he placed himself in that position because he had prior knowledge?'

'Damn it, I don't know how you sleep at night. I bet you're always lookin' under the bed.'

She grinned. 'And in the wardrobe.'

'Well, settin' all that to one side, I was about to say that we've got a walk of fifty yards or so. That gunman could still be hanging around. Stay alert, finger on the trigger.'

Some of the late-night drinkers who'd been disturbed by the gunfire were now unhitching their horses from the saloon's rail and riding out of town, hurriedly, in both directions. One of them called a hoarse 'good night' as he rode past Makin. The marshal waved a hand in acknowledgement, and went into his office. When Gallant and Melody Lake followed him in, he was already behind the desk in what was now his swivel chair. Ed Logan, as Gallant had expected, was pacing the floor restlessly.

Gallant crossed the small room and leaned nonchalantly against the steel gun cabinet bearing the slightest of dents from the impact of his head. Melody dragged a chair away from the wall, placed it so she could see everyone in the room without painfully twisting her neck, and sat down. The shotgun she placed across her thighs, muzzles pointing anywhere, nowhere, but remaining a potent threat.

'This,' the town councillor said as they settled, 'is getting to be a habit – and not a good one.'

CHAPTER EIGHT

'Not too sure if you're referring to yours, or mine,' Gallant objected, 'but, damn me, I'm getting miffed at the continual slurs, the blackening of my unstained character. Logan, I cannot in any way be blamed for this shooting.'

'I beg to differ. I was at my window, smoking a last cigar. I saw that man clearly. . . .'

'Aitken,' Gallant said.

'Yes, well, that name means nothing to me, but he crossed the street from the saloon, heading for the hotel. As you're Ma English's sole resident. . . .'

'No.' Melody Lake shook her head. 'He's not.'

Logan looked at her with a frown, as if noticing her for the first time. Continuing, he said, 'Well, all right. But, Gallant, the intention of this man Aitken must have been to talk to you – for some damn reason – so while not directly to blame for his death, you must admit to being somehow involved.'

'Involved in what? Care to be more specific?'

'You know damn well what I'm talking about.'

'He admits nothing,' Melody Lake said, 'and if you're going to let fly with accusations, we're getting out of here.'

Now Logan looked hard at her. 'And you are?'

Melody smiled at the councillor, but it was the cold smile of a predator, someone who would eat him for breakfast.

'I'm a lawyer. My name is Lake. I'm on my way to Yuma to join Edison, Young and Grey.'

'I know them. A respected old firm.' His smile was one of disbelief. 'Surely they're not taking you on as partner?'

'This is not about me.'

'Oh, but it is. Your career is on a knife edge. I saw a man shot down by an unknown gunman, after which a young woman fired a shotgun across a public thoroughfare, recklessly, without any thought for the safety of Gila Bend citizens. You were within town limits. I could have you prosecuted.'

'My,' Melody mocked, 'what big sharp teeth you have.'

'Damn you. . . .'

'Look, Logan,' Dan Makin cut in, 'present company's no place for expletives, and talk of prosecution is downright foolish. Gallant was in the street, out in the open, getting his hands bloody tending to a downed man. Lake was laying down covering fire, for that she deserves some credit. Hell, with a slice of luck she would have brought down that gunman. Going after her is wasting time. . . .'

'You're treading a fine line, Makin. A badge handed

out can just as easily be taken away.'

'Leaving this town where, exactly? Waiting for another drifter who happens to be passing through?' Makin grimaced apologetically at Gallant, then slammed his hands palm down on the desk and leaned forward. 'Logan, I was Owen's deputy for all of his time in office. Maybe that's my calling, the always dependable second string. If you want the opinion of a dependable deputy, your big mistake was sacking Gallant.'

'I resigned,' Gallant said before Logan could explode and angrily sack the current incumbent. 'With no regrets, then or now because, damn me, this problem grows more intriguin' by the hour. I'm a wily bird, and not having a badge gives me the freedom to get into all manner of scrapes with unpredictable consequences, which serves to keep a man on his toes. Results up to now have been spectacular – says he with his usual commendable modesty – but, as the talk seems to have drifted towards badges of one kind or another. . .'

He was digging into his pocket as he spoke, and finding the badge he'd taken from Aitken, he tossed it to Logan. It spun, flashed in the lamplight.

'Name on the back suggests the badge was taken from Owen,' Gallant said as Logan examined the circular piece of tin. 'It doesn't say how that was managed.'

'Because it didn't happen,' Logan said dismissively. 'Owen's badge at the time of his death was that of the Gila Bend marshal, later worn by you, now by Makin.

Owen could have lost this badge at any time in the years since he left the Texas Rangers.'

'Well, that ties in with Aitken's story of buying it from a Houston jeweller. But, as Dan Makin's already pointed out, we're wasting time discussing badges and the sins of fascinatin', feisty young female lawyers. Two men hanged a drunken killer name of Foster. I'm willing to bet it was one of those same men who put a rifle bullet in Aitken's skull.'

'They're killing their own,' Melody Lake said, and smiled somewhat dismissively at Logan's exclamation of disbelief. 'They are, or were, all members of the same lawless band. Those two – Foster and Aitken – were each given a task. They weren't up to the job, and paid the price.'

'Matches my ideas,' Gallant said, 'but how many of that band's left, I wonder.'

'No way of knowing. And most of what I've said is speculation.'

'But you do seem to know far too much for someone who's just hit town,' Logan said. 'How and when did you get here?'

'By the stage, a couple of days before Gallant rode in,' Lake said, and now it was Born Gallant trying to stop his jaw from dropping. 'I kept my head down, my long hair up under my hat, wore men's clothing and moved in shadows like a scavenging fox. Why would anyone notice little old me? There was far too much going on in a town that spends most of its life dozing in the hot sun. Clutching his notebook, scribbling madly, Stick McCrae would have been in his element.'

It was immediately clear to Gallant that Melody's mention of the Dodge City journalist's name worried Logan. Understandable, perhaps. Town councillors are minor politicians, and all politicians are fair game for those who work for the nation's newspapers. But wasn't McCrae still in Los Alamos? Well, perhaps not, perhaps now it was Yuma. And yet. . . .

He became aware of a dragging silence, of Logan's tense scrutiny.

'Recent events in El Dorado, written up so lucidly by McCrae, mean that all of us here have heard of him,' Gallant said softly. 'But McCrae's not in this room, so talk of him is more time wasted.'

Briefly he met Melody Lake's dark-eyed gaze, and saw something there that quickened his pulse. To Dan Makin he said, 'You say your deputy's out on his rounds?'

'The gunfire will have drawn him in. By now he'll be with the undertaker, Eli Gaunt.'

'Well, what those of us present have to do, and fast, is come up with intelligent ideas. You'll recall, Logan, that out at Boot Hill I asked you to work on figuring out what might happen next, because sure as eggs is eggs there's trouble brewing – if you'll excuse mixed metaphors. Later, Marshal Owen's brother said that, in his opinion, the only thing likely to attract outlaws to this lazy little Arizona town is all the gold and green money locked away in the bank's safe. '

He looked around at the listeners, raised an eyebrow, waited for comment.

'Where is he now, Owen's brother?' Logan said.

'Camping out in woods close to the river.'

'Well, if he's right about the bank,' Logan said, 'then we'll put a stop to any attempts at armed robbery.'

'We?'

'It's you doing all the talking. Let's see if you can back up talk with action, live up to your reputation. The bank opens at nine sharp, every weekday morning. Tomorrow I want John Martin, the owner, to have company, armed to the teeth.'

'And indeed he will. Two of us there, but well hidden,' Gallant said with a grin. He glanced across at Melody Lake, saw her almost imperceptible nod and went on, 'Your favourite lawyer will go in with Martin to a table behind the tellers. A scattering of ledgers, balance sheets she appears to be working on, will all serve to hide her trusty shotgun.'

'No matter what Logan says,' Dan Makin said, with a sideways glance at the councillor, 'surely you can't be involved? If it's the same two men who broke Foster out of jail and strung him up, you'll be recognized.'

'And you may be a stranger to them, but you're a married man with a pregnant wife,' Gallant said. 'Sorry, laddie, but there's certain to be shooting and that counts you out of it.'

'So, moving on,' Ed Logan said impatiently, 'this is the sequence. Martin always gets to the bank an hour before opening time to prepare for the day ahead: eight o'clock. At that time the street's always quiet, and we'll be waiting outside when he arrives. That in itself will be unusual, so Martin will know at once that something's up. I'll put him in the picture. He's sure to agree to the plan. In position, inside the bank when it opens, you'll have the advantage of surprise. That early I doubt if there'll be any customers to get in the way, and with two of you there, ready, armed. . . .'

'Actually,' Melody Lake said, 'it's not two, but three, and the third man of the indefatigable triumvirate certainly won't be known.'

'Dash it all,' Gallant said into the silence, putting a quaver in his voice, 'too many shocks in the one day can do a chap an immense amount of harm, don't you know? Here's me believing the feller to be in Los Alamos, Yuma, or some point in between, and unless I'm making a complete ass of myself I understand you to mean. . . .'

'And you're right,' Melody Lake said, rolling her eyes at his play-acting. 'I already told you I arrived the day before you, Gallant. But Stick McCrae, bless him, has been here in Gila Bend for a whole seven days.'

CHAPTER NINE

'By now I'd have expected to have heard from Eugene Owen.'

'Owen's brother, the man from Boot Hill, the saloon, and now camping on the Gila.'

'You know too much.'

'So I've been told.'

'Then where is McCrae?'

'Here and there,' Melody Lake said. 'Out and about.'

'Ha.' Born Gallant grinned. He'd beaten her. Posed a question she couldn't answer. But as she had clearly been watching *his* every move for a full twenty-four hours, then he'd bet a pound to a penny that McCrae was doing the same. Which made him a useful ally to have, always observing, lurking in the background ready to pounce.

Melody was watching him, highly amused.

'Out and about,' she said, 'as in riding along the banks of the Gila looking for that young man, Owen. I said yesterday there'd be three of us defending the bank, but four would be better.'

'So . . . let's hope they get here in time for the fun and games.'

It was seven-thirty the following morning. They'd emerged bleary-eyed from their separate rooms in Ma English's hotel, stepped gingerly down the steps that had featured so much in the previous night's action, then knocked with restraint on the door of the café. But Sally Adair, another who started the day early, was already in the kitchen firing up the stove. She'd let them in, hair damp, cheeks flushed, and when she'd happily responded to their request, they'd worked their way through steaming plates of fried ham, eggs, potatoes, following Gallant's usual dictum that a man – or a woman, he'd said, grinning at Lake – eats when he can, not when he must.

Now they were sitting back enjoying a second cup of coffee, and passing the time with talk that would take them through the next fifteen minutes, at the end of which Ed Logan was due to appear.

Incongruously, the American arms 12-gauge shotgun with its barrels shortened was propped against the table where Melody Lake was sitting, and a Winchester repeating rifle alongside Gallant. Or perhaps, Gallant thought, not incongruous: in this wild land where he was still a relative newcomer, lethal weapons at the breakfast table were probably commonplace.

'What d'you think of him?'

'Logan?' Gallant waggled his free hand palm down

in the horizontal plane. 'Undecided. Me, not him. Can't make him out. He takes me on, I slip up, he suggests I'm lying about the two men in white coats. Realizes that since I was locked in a cell I couldn't have hanged Foster, changes his tune – then, as you know, he again requests my help.'

'Typical small town councillor. Makes snap decisions, blames someone else when things head south. But there's intelligence in his eyes, and a wariness I don't understand.'

'Still harbouring suspicions? Well, strong males may laugh at the idea of womanly intuition. . . .'

'This little woman was imprisoned in a shack by a supposedly honourable politician. Logan is cut from the same shabby cloth.'

Gallant was still mulling over those words, and their possible portent, as Melody Lake thanked Sally and they moved outside and crossed the street to the bank.

Logan had been right about mornings at this time being quiet. Gila Bend wasn't exactly a ghost town, but the low mist drifting in off the river and hanging at street level in the still air turned houses and business premises into floating structures devoid of foundations, and the few citizens and mounted ranch hands already awake and about into bodies without legs.

Logan had walked the block or so from his rooms above the council offices. With him was the man called Earl Sedge. According to Logan he was the leader of the town council, and Logan's superior – his employer. He was standing back, another tall man. Gaunt face, nose like an eagle's beak and eyes as sharp as its claws, and a drooping cavalry moustache – but he was still, Gallant thought cynically, a man with the demeanour of a hunter doing a job suitable for a junior office boy.

Logan was now pacing restlessly in front of the bank. Same dark suit, but this morning he was wearing a pearl-grey Stetson. His jacket skirt was swept back on the right-hand side and caught behind the holster with its bone-handled six-gun.

Ready for instant action, Gallant wondered. Or was the six-gun exposed in that way to create an impression?

The tall councillor had slowed his pacing, and was watching their approach.

'Martin's not here yet,' he said.

Gallant shrugged his shoulders, indicated the mist, the mostly empty street. 'We're early. But what about the others, manager, clerks, tellers?'

'Martin is the manager, then there is one clerk, Mick Kelly, and a couple of tellers. Young women. They'll arrive ten minutes or so before opening. Martin likes a few minutes inside on his own. Maybe inhales deeply, smells money, puffs out his chest while basking in the atmosphere of the profitable business he's created through years of hard work.'

'Then we don't want to let the man down,' Gallant said. 'A robbery could wipe him out.'

'And would be bad for the town.'

'He been here long?'

'John? He arrived some five years back. Out of the blue, so to speak – he came from California, set up the bank. He's a respected citizen of Gila Bend.'

'On the council?'

Logan shook his head. 'Keeps himself to himself, at home with his wife. His house is in the style of a Mex' hacienda, but without cattle or fruit plantations.'

Gallant walked up the two stone steps, thumped the heavy oak door with his fist, rattled the knob; looked across to see Melody Lake, shotgun in the crook of her arm, disappearing up the littered alleyway to the right of the bank. She was back as he rejoined Logan, shaking her head.

'No windows on that side,' she said.

'Or the other,' Logan said, 'just these two at the front, and the back store room has one, very small. Dan Makin's staying in his office, as you recommended, but I've made damn sure young Rick Lyon is here, out back, mounted and armed.'

'So there's a back door?'

'Sure. Covered by Deputy Lyon. They go out that way, they're dead.'

Gallant nodded thoughtfully. 'Where will you be?'

'This is your show. Yours and Lake's. I'll leave you to it, wait with Marshal Makin in his office.' He jerked a thumb over his shoulder.

'Which leads me to think your plan needs a slight but important adjustment,' Gallant said.

Logan shook his head. 'A plan agreed by all. There's nothing wrong with it.'

'Any plan needs to be flexible,' Melody Lake said, immediately following Gallant's thinking. 'Two inside the bank, one out back. What about the front?'

66

Logan smiled, looked pointedly at Lake's shotgun, Gallant's Peacemaker. 'Once those bank robbers walk in, they're finished. Eli Gaunt's round the bend with his hearse, waiting for bodies to be carried out.'

'Yes,' Gallant said, 'he's already demonstrated a macabre ability to be in the wrong place at the right time, if you see what I mean – but shuttin' the stable door when the horse has bolted can make the best of men look foolish.'

'What the hell's that supposed to mean?'

'Lake's shotgun is a powerful weapon, but of little use if there's a couple of hysterical tellers between her and the robbers.

'So which of us is looking foolish? Wasn't it your idea for Lake to go in with you?'

'Yes, and now it's me changin' the plan. I'm putting myself across the street – first floor, high window, Winchester repeater – so if things do go wrong inside the bank that's the back and front doors covered.'

'Well, it worked for Aitken's killer,' Logan acknowledged. He looked at Lake. 'But didn't you say your friend McCrae would be involved?'

'He rode up the Gila looking for Eugene Owen. He's not back, and we're running out of time, and as you've decided to make yourself scarce I'd say Gallant's got it right.'

Logan was nodding slowly, ignoring the young lawyer's implied insult but clearly not happy.

'He was right about the scattergun being a bad choice for inside work, even more so now you're on your own. Give that double-barrelled monster to me,

67

Lake. You've got a six-gun?'

She nodded, handed the shotgun to Logan, briefly pulled open her light cotton jacket to display a Smith & Wesson Pocket .38 worn high in a soft leather holster.

'Excellent. I know you believe that by positioning myself in the jail I'm thinking of my own skin, but look at it this way. Even with you on the inside and both doors covered, things could go wrong. If they do, well, there's nothing better than a scattergun for bringing down a rider on a fast horse.'

'Last resort,' Gallant said, and nodded. 'But you must know any bank robber worth his salt would die laughin' at that five-shot pistol Lake's carryin'. Seems to me you're suggestin' she's inside only to protect Martin's staff – another last resort, that she's going to allow the bank robbery to proceed unhindered.'

Logan smiled. 'Why would I suggest anything? This is your plan now, Gallant. And I hate to admit it, but what you just said makes a whole lot of sense. Worked that way, Mick Kelly and the two tellers will be in no danger. They'll hand over the cash, the robbers will walk out the front door and you'll . . . well . . . you in that upstairs window, me down the street in the jail – let's see what happens.'

CHAPTER TEN

The bearded owner of the general store opposite the bank had already opened his premises, lit a lamp to dispel the morning gloom inside the store, and was stacking garments and leather goods on outside shelves, grain sacks against the wall. Gallant crossed the street, explained what he wanted, and was gratified when the man agreed to his request without hesitation. The first floor front room was empty apart from some boxes, he told Gallant. The window would open easily so there would be no need for broken glass.

Inside, they chatted for a few minutes. The store owner – a man called Gord Brown – then showed Gallant the way around the sales counter to the stairs, and asked only that when he came in with his rifle he didn't terrorize grey-haired old ladies. He was still chuckling at the joke when Gallant shook his hand and left.

Earl Sedge had left, striding back up the street to his office to conduct some kind of council business. Surprisingly, Melody Lake still had her shotgun, and

Ed Logan was outside the bank talking to an over-weight bald man in a black suit, shiny in patches: Mark Kelly, the clerk. The tellers were two young women in formal grey frocks. They were standing talking nearby.

'All set?'

Gallant nodded.

'Well, Martin is now long overdue,' Logan said. 'He holds the only keys, of course. Without him, his staff can't get in.'

'They're not the only ones.'

'The bank robbers?' Logan frowned. 'Yes, they're also overdue, and perhaps keeping the place locked up is the surest way of stopping a robbery.'

'Nobody gets hurt,' Gallant said, nodding, but he was talking absently, his attention elsewhere.

One of the young women had stopped talking to her friend and walked away, somewhat hesitantly. Her head was bent as she looked down. Then, hiking her skirt up almost to her knees, she crouched down and picked up something that she'd spotted lying half buried in the thick dust accumulated in the angle between the street and the bank's stone wall.

'Got it,' she said.

She stood up. Awkwardly off balance, she took a backward step, then lifted her hand. In the bright morning sunlight the object she held flashed brilliantly. Her hand was trembling with what might have been nervous excitement, or the onset of fear, because the shiny object was faintly jingling.

It was a big key ring, holding a number of iron keys.

'I saw it down there, winking in the sunlight, the bits

70

that weren't buried all shiny,' she said; and suddenly she changed hands and began scrubbing her palm fiercely on her frock's skirt. 'At first I thought it was broken glass,' she said in a choked voice, 'but, this, oh God, look at them, Mick. . . .'

Her face a mask of horror, she flung the keys at Kelly.

He caught them, grimaced, took one glance at what he was holding and turned to Logan.

'They're the keys to the bank, but. . . .' He shook his head and his face had gone pale. 'They're dusty, of course, but sticky too,' he said. 'I think . . . I think it's blood.'

'Get the place opened up.'

Kelly seemed horrified at the thought. He looked again at the keys, then reluctantly nodded at Logan. With all the eagerness of a doomed man mounting the gallows he went up the two stone steps and selected the largest of the keys. He inserted it, turned the lock.

The two girls hesitated, exchanged apprehensive glances.

'Take the day off, both of you,' Logan called. 'Go home, now. And keep your mouths shut.'

'And you, Kelly, stop where you are,' Gallant said, and brushed past Logan. Lake was also moving forward, approaching the steps. Kelly, about to push open the door, stopped and looked back.

'I know this is your place of work,' Gallant said, 'but have you any idea what you might find in there? You know the stickiness on your hands is drying blood. It scared you half to death – and that's an unintentional,

71

ugly pun that I hope isn't a portent.'

The clerk was struggling to recover his composure, looking from the keys to Gallant, beginning to consider possible explanations.

'Martin is always the last to leave,' he said. 'He locks up. Blood on the keys, the keys lying in the dust, suggests he cut himself, a nasty accident, either before or after he locked the bank.'

'No. You're desperate to come up with a safe, sensible reason for those dropped keys,' Gallant said, 'but you *know* it's daylight when Martin locks up. The street would have been busy, the general store opposite still open. I was over there a few minutes ago, spoke to Gord Brown. He's an observant chap. I'd say he sees Martin leaving, every day, sets his watch by the man's punctual timekeeping. Brown would surely have noticed him acting strangely, stumbling, holding a bloody hand.'

Ed Logan was listening, now shaking his head. 'This is getting us nowhere. The door's unlocked, anyone could walk in and we're expecting a raid on the bank. . . .'

'That's done, finished, over with.'

The silence following Gallant's blunt statement was almost painful. The clerk looked stunned. For some reason known only to himself Logan was clearly struggling to control his emotions. His jaw was tight, his expression blank, unreadable. He stared hard at Gallant, then turned away and gestured Kelly down from the steps.

'There're people across the street watching this,

and you've got customers arriving,' he said, indicating a businessman in a serge suit, a ranch hand looking over at the group as he dismounted from his horse. 'Tell them the bank's closed for the day, unforeseen circumstances. Then do like your tellers, go home. . . .'

'But the keys. . . .'

'I'll take charge of them, keep them safe, once we find out. . . .'

He was still talking when Gallant nodded to Melody Lake, pushed open the unlocked door and led the way into the bank.

In the eerie silence they could hear the clerk passing on the bad news to his customers. The voice was indistinct, muffled: Gallant had shut the door behind them. Now, the two high windows flanking the door were letting in shafts of bright morning sunlight in which motes floated like fireflies. The light stroked the dusty floor, hit the shiny tops of the polished wooden counters, sent reflections dancing on the wood-panelled back wall, in which a single door stood ajar.

'The back room,' Melody Lake said.

'Yes. Probably where they store paperwork and so on. Also, somewhere to keep a big iron safe with its neat stacks of banknotes away from prying eyes. Any blood spilled,' Gallant said, 'will have been spilled out there, in that back room.'

'Damn,' Lake said. 'Does that explain why we're standing here like wallflowers at a wedding bash? If so, since when have dead bodies sent us into a blue funk?' Another swift glance. 'You think it's Martin, don't you?'

'Who else? His bank, his keys. And I'm also wondering why his wife's not in town, acting high and mighty rather than distressed, looking for a husband who's stayed out all night.'

But now he was talking to Lake's back. Tired of talk that was delaying the inevitable, she'd headed for the counter and had already lifted the hinged flap and was through to the staff area behind the counters. By the time Gallant had up and followed she was approaching the door to the back room.

'Melody,' he called softly.

She stopped, waited, shotgun in the crook of her arm.

'No need for that scatter thing,' he said, 'and no need for you to go in first. A man's job, don't you know? Needs a fellow who's seen it all in damnably hot climes, faced bearded mountain men in white robes wielding curved knives. . .'

He was talking the usual nonsense while walking, brushing past her with unaccustomed roughness and on without hesitation into the back room. And there he did stop; held out a stiff arm to block Melody Lake as she tried to come through.

'Not Martin, after all,' he said. 'Although that, too, is wrong, it's just not the Martin we expected.'

The banker's wife – Gallant assumed it was her – was lying on her back. Grey-haired, barefoot, she wore nothing but a dressing gown covering a thin night-dress. Her eyes, glazed, were staring sightlessly at the high ceiling. Her throat had been cut. Her clothing was soaked in blood from neck to waist.

She was lying on the floor in front of the safe. Its door was wide open. There was nothing on the shelves but disturbed paperwork, a couple of leather-bound ledgers tossed carelessly to the very back. A single dollar bill had floated free, unnoticed when the robbers made their getaway. It was resting like a fallen autumn leaf at the dead woman's bloody throat.

'Suddenly, all becomes clear,' Melody Lake said softly.

She'd ignored his stiff-armed barrier and followed him in, as he'd known she would. In such trying circumstances, he found her indomitable spirit truly amazing – but that was Melody Lake. There was a rough pine table in the middle of the room. She dropped the shotgun on it with a clatter, brushed back her dark hair, folded her arms. Her eyes were intent on him, and he knew she was waiting for him to put into words the events that had led to a successful bank robbery, a woman's violent death.

'They went to Martin's house in those hours before dawn when humans are at their weakest,' Gallant said, trying not to look at the dead woman. 'Broke in there with ease, instead of here in town when daylight would have made entry and robbery more difficult, more dangerous. They disturbed two people in their bed, not young, at their lowest ebb. No doubt they were threatening, loud and violent. They brought the woman here to open up because the man might have been hard to handle, whereas she would have been terrified, submissive.'

'No, I think they had no choice,' Melody Lake said.

'Martin would have resisted when they broke in. He was put to the sword.'

'We English blue bloods have a way with words; it appears to be catching.' He smiled briefly. 'But that sword wouldn't have fallen until they'd made damn sure they had the keys, and that his wife knew the safe's combination.'

'True. But if he didn't die in the initial assault, then to kill him without reason, when they had what they needed, was cold-blooded murder.'

'If they did,' Gallant said. 'We don't know how the story unfolded. But it's becoming clear that's the way this outlaw band operates, and tells us what the unlucky man to go out to the house will find. The latest proof of their ruthless methods lies at our feet. She gave them the safe's combination, they got the money, and so she was no longer of any use.'

'Christ! And it could all have been done without a drop of blood being spilled,' Lake said, shaking her head in disbelief. 'They got the keys and the numbers when they were at the house. They didn't need to kill the banker or bring his wife into town.'

'We'll never know for sure what went on,' Gallant said, taking a last glance at the banker's dead wife and turning towards the door. 'These fine, brave fellows are never going to be taken alive. They'll die in a hail of bullets rather than face that gallows.' His back was turned to her when he said, under his breath but fiercely nevertheless, 'And, by God, I'll make sure they do.'

He knew he was being a cad by walking out ahead of

Melody Lake, forgetting his manners and all that, but, dammit all, this latest killing was sickening. The drunken Foster had killed and was destined to hang, so good riddance. Aitken was an unknown, but he'd been armed and gunning for Gallant. But Martin's wife . . .?

'Gallant, give me the keys.'

He stopped, swung round. Instead of following him she had swept up the shotgun and was standing with her other hand out.

'We're done here,' she said, 'and that deputy's out back.'

'Lyon. Yes, I know. . . .'

'I'll tell him it's over, give him the keys. He can ride around and fetch that ghoulish undertaker and his black chariot. When they've taken care of the body, Lyon can lock this place.'

She caught the keys and he watched her go to the back door, with difficulty turn the rusty key that was in the lock – she had her hands full, and it was a door not often opened – and step out into the shade cast by the stone building. He heard her call to Lyon, then turned and walked out of the room that stank of blood, through the bank's main business area and across to the front door.

He stepped out it into dazzling sunlight that was painful to the eyes and turning Gila Bend's main street into a fiery, dusty canyon. The bank's door he left wide open. No sense closing it when there was nothing left inside worth stealing, the keys were with Lyon, so. . . .

The town was now wide awake. There were plenty of people about – some riders, a wagon or two – and most were casting curious glances at the bank as they went about their business. Gord Brown was standing outside his general store, talking to a man of his own age. He'd watched Gallant come out into the sunlight and now lifted both hands, palms up, in a questioning gesture.

Gallant shook his head and went down the steps. He barely noticed the young deputy, Lyon, as he rode out of the alley alongside the bank and turned his horse towards the bend in the street that was hiding the town's ever watchful undertaker. His whole attention was focused on the baking hot street, in particular on the area in front of the jail.

In that charnel house of a back room, Gallant had truly believed that things could not get worse. He'd been wrong.

A man was riding towards Gallant. He was astride a fine sorrel mare. The ragged, riderless chestnut behind him was lathered but walking easily on a lead rope attached to the man's saddle horn.

'Stick McCrae,' Gallant said softly. 'And if I'm not mistaken, that horse my old friend is bringing into town belongs to a man last known to be camping on the banks of the Gila.'

Melody Lake had come up behind him. She stepped close, placed a hand on his shoulder.

'It was tough, but it's going to get tougher, young man,' she said; and she bumped him with her hip, met his glance and raised eyebrows with a cold smile that quickly faded. 'A riderless horse. The name of Eugene Owen can be added to a list that's going to get much longer,' she said. 'You know, Gallant, this town and its environs are taking on the deathly stench of a Civil War battlefield when the guns of both sides have fallen silent.'

CHAPTER ELEVEN

An hour later. An hour to go before midday.

Born Gallant and Stick McCrae were riding out of Gila Bend in an easterly direction. A little way out of town the river took a sharp loop to the north. Looking to their left, they could see the last wraiths of the morning's river mist being dissipated by the sun. On the fertile land within that loop of the river, where some shelter from the heat and the hot dry winds was afforded by stands of cottonwoods and aspens, bank owner John Martin had built a modest house. And there, for more than ten years, he had lived a comfortable, tranquil life with his wife.

All that had been changed by one night of bloody horror.

Ed Logan, along with Marshal Dan Makin, had listened in stunned silence as Gallant and Melody Lake had walked up to the jail and described the grisly scene in the bank's back room – had then stared blankly when Stick McCrae pushed open the street door and walked into the tense silence. Logan, a man they assumed was accustomed to a routine desk job in a town where violence was judged by the number of shots fired by Saturday night drunks, appeared to be in deep shock. When Gallant introduced McCrae, Makin had nodded a polite welcome, but the town councillor had been unable to respond. Instead, he had ducked his head and mumbled something about informing his council colleagues, had slammed the door on his hurried way out. From the jail he could be seen walking like a man condemned across the street to the offices beneath his own accommodation.

Melody Lake, still lugging her shotgun but with obvious irritation – it had been nothing but an encumbrance during a non-violent morning – had been thinking ahead to the tiring stagecoach journey to Yuma and her first meeting with her new legal partners. She had informed Gallant that she would be in touch, and had left the jail shortly after Logan.

The Yuma stage would be coming through at noon.

Dan Makin, reluctant to leave the jail while his deputy was still out assisting undertaker Eli Gaunt, had asked Gallant and McCrae to ride out to the Martin house and check on the banker's health. They had listened to his directions, collected their horses from the town's livery barn, and set off on the reasonably short ride.

'It ain't likely to be too good,' McCrae said now, looking across at Gallant. 'What Makin was saying about Martin's health,' he explained as Gallant looked blank.

'Yes, sorry old chap, you're absolutely right but I was

fascinated by these two fellers comin' towards us. Don't know why, possibly because back in Kansas, Mexicans were thin on the ground.'

The two riders split up as they approached. They were both wearing traditional Mexican clothing with the characteristic, broad-brimmed sombrero, reds and yellows garish in the bright sunlight. They nodded and grinned broadly as they rode by on either side of Gallant and McCrae, heading towards town. Their flashing teeth were made to look extra white by their dark, flowing moustaches.

'But getting' away from Martin for the moment,' Gallant went on, facing front again, 'I'm still waitin' to hear about young Owen.'

'Something must have disturbed him,' McCrae said. 'He'd tried to crawl out of his blankets, almost made it but his feet got tangled and he took a bullet in the face. I dragged his body into the woods – wrapped in that blanket roll – and did what I could to cover it with rocks, brushwood.'

'He told me he'd camp on the banks of the river, I figured it was on this side of town. . . .'

'Over there,' McCrae said, waving left. 'We're quite close.'

'Mm. Bit hazy, lot of dust hanging in the air – you noticed?'

'Over the trail? Well, in this climate, and there being no wind today, what d'you expect it to do?'

Gallant grinned. 'Point taken. But what I was driving at is that hanging dust means riders passing to and fro – and I don't see any.'

'You just saw two happy-go-lucky vaqueros. Anyway, this trail goes all the way from Yuma in the west to, well, pretty well any place in an easterly direction.' He cast a questioning glance at Gallant. 'Any point to this conversation?'

'Not too sure,' Gallant said, and he reached forward, absently patted his horse's silky neck. 'Close to Owen's overnight camp, you say,' he mused, 'but aren't we also getting pretty close to Martin's house?'

'Ah, no. If you're suggesting it was a disturbance in that house that woke Owen, he'd have had more than enough time to get out of his blankets.'

'I'm thinking more of the man who cut the woman's throat in the Gila Bend bank,' Gallant said. 'Always supposin' his partner stayed in the house with Martin, the wife killer would need to come back this way, saddlebags stuffed with a lot of paper money. Middle of the night, yes, all on his lonesome – but if he rode back from town along the riverbank so's to keep from bein' seen, it's possible he almost rode straight over the sleeping Owen.'

'You always were one for making the simple more complicated,' McCrae said. 'Owen's dead, Gallant, and in a little less than five minutes we'll be saying the same about bank owner, John Martin.'

They rode the rest of the way without talking. Gallant was deep in thought, but those thoughts were disturbed as soon as they left the trail, rode through a thin stand of trees to a small clearing and saw the white-painted timber house bathed in sunlight, a small corral, and an outbuilding close to the house that was

83

little more than a timber shed.

'Damn it,' Gallant said softly, and jerked his horse back to a slow walk, instinctively reaching a reassuring hand to his Colt Peacemaker.

'Two horses at the hitch rail,' McCrae said, 'and I can see one in that small corral. That one looks classy, it'll belong to the Martins. But these two? They belong to rough riders, not to a bank owner or his wife.'

'Visualizing what must have gone on,' Gallant said, 'I had that killer hot-footin' it back from town with the cash, then him and his partner heading for the border at a rate of knots – any border you care to name. But now. . . ?'

'Exactly,' McCrae said. 'Hanging about waiting for the law to visit them doesn't make sense.'

'What makes even less sense is us sitting out here in the open when there could be two men in there watching us over the sights of repeating rifles.'

'There's nothing in that house,' McCrae said, 'but death.'

'Doesn't explain the horses,' Gallant said, and he swung down from the saddle, left the roan's reins trailing in the dust and jogged up the path to the front door.

McCrae was up with him as he crossed the gallery.

'Front door opened with finesse,' he remarked, pointing at the shattered lock.

Gallant's eyes were everywhere, his ears tuned to pick up any sound.

Nothing. He pushed open the door, stepped inside. Sniffed. Closed his eyes.

'Christ,' he said softly.

'A slaughterhouse, the stench of blood, and didn't you say the dead woman in the bank was in her night clothes?' McCrae looked at Gallant for confirmation, and at once made a run for the stairs.

There he slowed. They went up cautiously, silently, placing their feet with care, which was ridiculous because Gallant agreed with McCrae: there was nobody alive to hear their footsteps. We've drawn our guns, he thought, but if we shoot we'll be shooting the dead. And he watched as McCrae turned towards the front bedroom, pushed fully open the half-closed door – and stopped.

The lean, tough journalist turned to stare at Gallant. His face was pale. He spread his hands in disbelief as Gallant grabbed his shoulder, shook it, then pushed his way past him and into the room.

'Three in a bed,' he said, feeling a sudden desperate need to fill the deathly silence.

'And all of them dead.'

'Sounds like we're auditioning for vaudeville,' Gallant said. 'Make a fine pair, don't we, talking sublime nonsense in the presence of tragedy? Martin's the older feller in the middle. The other two. . . .'

'Well, so now we know for sure they weren't looking at us over the sights of a repeating rifle. They did the last of their looking some time ago – but what's with the long duster coats?'

'For recognition. That's how they were dressed when they broke Foster from the jail. Someone's saying it's over, the men who freed a killer then strung him up are themselves now dead. But under that ripe stink of blood there's another smell in here, and this one's tellin' me a different story, one you'd think they'd want to keep secret,' Gallant said. 'Don't want to be disrespectful to Mexicans as a race, but aren't those characters aficionados of food hot enough to burn the tongue from your mouth, eat their beef or tortillas laced with hot chilli peppers?'

'Fond of knife-work, too,' McCrae said.

The white sheets of the bed, and the scruffy duster coats, were stiff with drying blood. Martin and his wife, Gallant thought. Two had their throats cut in the space of a few hours. The fellers wearing dusters? At a quick glance, both had been shot in the back of the head. So, taken by surprise – but why dead, why kill them? What the hell was going on?

'These are the two men who robbed the bank,' Gallant said softly, more to himself than to McCrae. 'That's their horses out there. But the two men are dead, and that tells me the stolen money that was in those saddlebags is long gone.'

Sickened, he turned his back on the blood-soaked double bed, walked to the window. He slid it open, took a deep breath of clean air, gazed into the distance, then let his gaze drift closer. Smiled crookedly, he shook his head.

'And you know exactly where it's gone,' McCrae was saying. 'We watched two happy-go-lucky vaqueros ride by with big hats and even bigger grins. You can bet your life the knives in their scabbards were stained with blood, a couple of cartridges missing from a gunbelt, their saddle-bags stuffed with money. They left the trail before Gila Bend, and it's fifty miles to Ajo, maybe another twenty to the Mex border. By now they'll be halfway home.'

'No, they won't.' Gallant turned to McCrae. 'If you're keen to lay a bet, don't wager your life. Those vaqueros with their sunny smiles watched us pass, gave us time, then doubled back. They're outside, Stick – and it's possible the only way out of this place is through that busted front door.'

CHAPTER TWELVE

'During the bloody siege of Badajoz, in 1812, the Duke of Wellington lost almost five thousand of his men,' Gallant said in a conversational tone. 'Twenty per cent. It was a bloodbath, because attacking a citadel, a fortress where defenders are high up and protected by stone walls, is always a risky business.'

'This is not the Iberian Peninsula,' McCrae said, 'and these walls are not stone.'

'Principle's the same.'

'What are they doing?'

Gallant, careful to stand to one side, was still looking out of the window into dazzling sunshine.

'They're down off their horses. One's spotted me. He's swept off his sombrero. Damn feller's got the infernal cheek to give me a mocking bow.'

'The other?'

'He jogged at an angle towards the house. I can't see him.'

'Being trapped inside a timber building,' McCrae said, 'always does make me uneasy.'

'Happen often?'

'This is the first time, but the thought's always been there. And that outbuilding alongside the house worries me. Storeroom, wouldn't you say?'

Gallant nodded, suddenly serious.

'Following your line of thinking, a family would need somewhere to keep the oil for their lamps. And an excellent way of obliterating all traces of a crime is by burning the bodies. Dead or alive.'

He'd turned on his heel and was moving away from the window as he spoke. McCrae, quick to react, was ahead of him. They both piled out of that gruesome bedroom, away from the raw reek of spice and blood. Guns drawn, they reached the top of the stairs, started down. As fast as they moved they had covered no more than two or three steps when there was a loud bang. The open front door had been kicked wide. The second Mexican was on the gallery, a big shape blocking the bright sun. He was holding a small oildrum. McCrae was the first to reach the downstairs passageway. The Mexican saw him, drew back his arms, and as McCrae ran towards him he tipped the drum and flung the liquid contents into the house.

The whole operation was well planned.

McCrae staggered back, clothes and face soaked in oil, half blind. He blocked Gallant's advance, knocked him back against the wall. The Mexican tossed the empty oil drum away. It clattered across the gallery. Then in one smooth movement he drew his six-gun, dropped to one knee and fired two shots. The pistol's muzzle was pointing down, inches away from the oil-drenched floor. The double muzzle flash ignited the oil. Flames licked rapidly towards McCrae.

At the same time, over the head of his kneeling *compañero*, the first Mexican loosed a fusillade of shots from McCrae's Winchester.

Gallant, both hands on McCrae's shoulders, desperately pulling him back from the advancing flames, felt the shock of lead hitting the newspaperman's body. Suddenly he was lurching backwards. His fingers were hooked into McCrae's wet shirt. He was struggling to stay on his feet while holding up what had become a dead weight.

'Leave me,' McCrae croaked. 'Get out, I'm done for.'

'Shut up. Save your breath.'

The flames had reached Gallant's boots. His heels banged against the bottom stair. Go up?

On his own he'd make it, but not carrying McCrae. Besides, going up meant nothing more than delaying the inevitable: an agonizing death in a burning house. And already McCrae's clothing was smouldering, about to burst into flames.

The heat in that downstairs hallway was intolerable. It had driven back the Mexican who had started the blaze – but he had never intended to enter the house. The flames would be sucked upwards, that was the nature of fire in enclosed spaces with stairwells. That updraft would greedily draw oxygen from the air but give Gallant precious seconds to drag the groaning McCrae to the back door – if there was one.

Ignoring McCrae's distress he picked him up bodily

and draped him over his shoulder. At once he felt warm blood on his face, his hands. Spitting, he went past the stairs, heading for the rear of the house. He kicked open a door, found himself in a kitchen. Used a push from his backside to close the door behind him. The roar of the fire became muffled. Black, oily smoke had curled along the hall and reached the kitchen, but breathing was possible.

One small window. The corral, trees, distant hills.

A Mexican, on horseback. Watching the back of the house, rifle held at the port. The rising column of smoke from the fire was already casting a shadow over the land.

'I'm putting you down, Stick.'

A grunt. Gallant awkwardly lowered McCrae. He let him slip into a slumped sitting position with his back against a steel cupboard, winced as the newspaperman's head banged against the door.

'Sorry,' Gallant said automatically, eyeing with dismay the blood-soaked shirt, the pants wet and blood-red down one thigh. The wounded man's face was white. He'd closed his eyes. Their lids looked transparent.

Somehow, Gallant had hung on to his Peacemaker. The loops of his gunbelt held spare shells, but in a fierce gunfight there would be no time to reload. The only way out was through the back door. By now both Mexicans would be there, mounted, waiting.

Gallant looked back at the door leading to the hall. By the sound of it the fire had reached the upper floor. It had also advanced along the hall. The intense heat was causing the door's panels to split. Smoke was seeping through. Old paintwork was blistering. Going out that way was impossible, yet to open the back door was to commit suicide.

Gallant knew that in such a situation two men were needed. Not to even the odds, but to work together to overcome the impossible. If storming a citadel was a formidable task for an army, breaking out of that citadel and through the army holding siege, armed with nothing more than a hand gun, was. . . .

Suddenly, Gallant looked at McCrae. At the steel locker. He was remembering the jail, his own pistol-whipping, which had ended with his head creating a dent in a steel door. A door like this one.

Damn it.

'Stick. . . .'

The wounded man was unconscious.

Gallant took him by the shoulders, dragged him to one side, eased him down sideways. Hastily he tried the steel door. Unlocked. The hinges were stiff, but gave to Gallant's fierce tug. And then there was a moment of fierce exultation. It was Martin's armoury, the weapons he had collected over the years to protect his wife, the house. He had two old Henry repeaters, a heavy pistol that could be an early Colt Navy. But Gallant had eyes only for the gleaming shotgun. It was a Remington 10-gauge with long double barrels.

Gallant grabbed it, checked the loads, ran to the back door. He dragged it open, leaped back out of a possible line of fire and let it slam back against the wall and remain wide open. Then he ran to the window.

Yes. The two Mexicans were there. Both on horseback. Both staring intently at the open door, rifles at the ready as they waited for the trapped man to be driven out by the raging inferno.

Or the trapped *men* to be driven out, Gallant thought; they couldn't know for certain that the shots fired from the front door had brought down McCrae. The advantage lay with the Mexicans, in position and numbers – but they couldn't know that.

Also – another plus for Gallant – like inexperienced cavalrymen disobeying basic rules of combat, they had their horses close enough together for their heavy wooden stirrups to clash.

At the window Gallant used the shotgun's muzzle to shatter the glass. The noise was loud, even above the roar of the flames – it could fool the Mexicans into believing the fire had spread into the kitchen. Gallant waited, out of sight but able to see. He counted to two, to three, to four, let the tension build as the Mexicans snapped glances uncertainly from the unexplained open door to the shattered window, and back again. Then, on the count of ten, Gallant leaped to the window. He took a fast aim, which with a shotgun was all that was needed, and pulled both triggers. He was unbalanced. The double blast almost knocked him backwards. Without looking at what damage he'd caused he dropped the shotgun, ran to the door and leaped out.

One horse had wheeled away from the house, eyes rolling, terrified by the leaping flames and the shotgun's blast. But it was unable to run because the rider was down, his foot caught in the stirrup, his weight holding back the lunging horse. With one swift glance Gallant saw that the shotgun's double blast had damn near removed the man's head from his body.

The other Mexican was uninjured, but fighting to control his horse. Rough broken, poorly trained, it too was panicking, bucking madly, fighting the steel bit that was cutting its mouth as the Mexican dragged hard on the reins.

With all the time in the world and with fury carefully controlled, Gallant drew his Peacemaker, took a steady bead on the moving target and shot the Mexican out of his saddle.

Then with a heavy heart, he went back into the burning building for Stick McCrae.

CHAPTER THIRTEEN

'It was a case of getting out fast, or facing a fiery death,' Born Gallant said. 'I used a shotgun from the window on the first man, wounded the second with the Peacemaker. When he fell I went back into the house for you, then dragged you and the wounded Mex well clear of that blazing house. Exhausting work, don't you know. And you were no help at all.'

'I'll try to do better next time, sir,' McCrae said.

Gallant grinned. 'The Mexican was still alive. Had enough breath to speak, to spit in my face. The bank's money had gone. Before he and his pal rode back to the Martin house to deal with us, they'd handed all the stolen loot to another Mexican. The man pulling the strings, calling the shots.'

They were in Gallant's room in Ma English's Gila Bend rooming house, which she was proud to call a hotel. He was sitting on a straight chair close to the open window. A faint warm breeze was fluttering the dirt-grey net curtain. He'd let Stick McCrae sit on the bed, the most comfortable place in an uncomfortable room for a man still feeling the pain of his wounds.

'So,' McCrae said, 'that's not two Mexicans, but three – at the last count.'

'Involved here in Gila Bend, before, during and after a bank robbery? Yes. Which has set me wondering. White Americans doing a lot of the dirty work, but Mexicans dealing the cards. Why? I'd say the two Mexicans that came back to the Martin house were peasants enlisted as cannon fodder. Go there, do this, put your life on the line. That's what the third Mexican would have been saying. In the end he was clear and running, with a saddle-bag packed with banknotes.'

'Which puts Martin's money over the border into Mexico a full four weeks ago.'

'That long, yes. We know that feller left the day you damn near died. A lot of stolen money left Arizona, in the hands of a killer.'

'And you worked that out, how? If he was boss man, giving orders, wouldn't he be keeping his hands clean?'

'Killer's a reasonable assumption. I reckon when they handed the money to him he was riding away from Martin's house. When we got there, three men were dead. Also, it's like a deadly circle: men have died, then their killers have themselves been killed, and so on. A nasty trail of dead bodies, leading to the inevitable conclusion that there has to be one man left standing. And there was a lot of knifework. We're looking at a cold, cruel character hired by someone with power for that very quality. Get the cash, kill off anyone likely to spill the beans, then get out. As you pointed out, whoever and whatever he is, he's safely over the border.'

'A rich killer.'

'And out of the Gila Bend marshal's jurisdiction.' Gallant shrugged. 'I told Ed Logan everything, gave him the full story. There was nothing he could do but arrange for bodies to be carted to Boot Hill by Eli Gaunt, and buried without ceremony. Marshal Dan Makin's hands are tied, and Logan seemed to be reasoning that with Martin dead there was no point anyone going south of the border to chase Mexican shadows.'

'But that's now your intention?'

'Always was.'

'You think I'm up to it?'

'I have serious misgivings. You're the old Stick McCrae, but stuck with a limp. In need of support, so to speak. The Stick moniker takin' on a whole new meaning.'

'You saying I'll be in the way?'

Gallant stared out of the window. The banter sounded cruel – on his side, anyway – but that was not the intention. He and Stick always traded verbal blows. For Gallant, this return to that trading of insults reassured him that Stick McCrae was truly on the mend.

'Far from it,' he said, swinging away from the window, stepping off the hard chair and stretching. 'Even this side of the border I'm still a wayfarin' stranger, so Mexico's going to be like another planet. The red dust plains of Mars. I need help, Stick, and despite the cheap cracks I've been tossin' your way – one of my less attractive traits, by the way – you've never yet let me down.'

McCrae stretched his leg out from the bed, held it straight, let it bend at the knee.

'You know, I think you're wrong about the limp. This leg will be as good as new.'

'Or as good as the old one,' Gallant said. 'Well, miracles do happen. I rode into Gila Bend leading four horses and with you bleeding all down my shirt front from that shoulder wound. I thought you were dead. But here we are, gazing south to that distant Mexican border. The intention being to cross over and seek out the pueblo of San Miguel and, in the nearby foothills, a hacienda owned by a *caballero* called Diego Martinez.'

'You still haven't told me why. There was a bank robbery and more than one murder, but it's not our problem. Martin's dead, the bank has no money. Ed Logan's not interested. . . .'

'Melody Lake,' Gallant said, 'has her suspicions about our tall town councillor.'

'Logan?'

'I joked with her about womanly intuition, but I have to admit that man's behaviour has, at times, looked decidedly odd. Well, behaviour, no, but there was always something in that man's eyes. . . .'

'As Melody would say, that's not enough to convict a man in a court of law.'

'Look, one of my reasons for heading south is

because I made a fool of myself. Took on the job of town marshal with one prisoner safely locked up, and ended up looking like an ass. Can't allow that, Stick, old fruit. Makin' amends to myself is priority. Restorin' the old ego. Dustin' off the soiled reputation.'

'That means I'm a sorely wounded man tagging along to help repair an image that, frankly, has always been somewhere between the sublime and the ridiculous.'

Gallant grinned. 'Can't say that's not deserved! So put the second reason for heading south to something still personal, but more . . . I don't know, honourable? A feelin' of personal pain when I see a friend close to death. An aversion to allowin' killers to get off Scot free. And a question over why Mexicans were using white Americans. And who put 'em up to it?'

'Yes, that's a good point previously raised: why the bank at Gila Bend? And who had the Mexican connection?'

'That could be too easy. One man recently dead spent a lot of time in Nuevo Laredo. He was wearing a Texas Ranger badge.'

'Owen?'

'The only man we know fits the bill,' Gallant said. 'But I've been wondering why that kid shot him. One answer is he'd served his purpose, was of no more use. The one I prefer is that he had no purpose, but recognized someone. He sent to his brother for help, but he got here too late.'

'Sure, and we can say that the Mex who's now well over the border with his saddlebags stuffed with

Martin's cash could have been the man giving the killing order. But what if. . . .'

'Ah, yes,' Gallant said. 'What if there's someone there, in the background, some crafty character pulling a lot of strings, someone we've yet to get a sniff of?'

'And so now it's clear where this is leading.'

'I get the feeling,' Gallant said, 'that all this thieving and killing is being organized by someone who knows Gila Bend inside out. Can sit back and watch comings and goings. Actions and reactions. Plan accordingly. Get rich without straining a muscle. And that isn't my idea of a Texas Ranger who became a small town marshal.'

'Hence Melody's suspicions, your trust in womanly intuition and the look in a man's eyes. So Logan's there, a shady character in the background – but you still haven't told me *where* we're going.'

'Many years ago, a certain Don Diego lost a lot of money. Lost is the wrong word. He was robbed. I got this story in laboured gasps from the dying Mexican who spat in my face. He reckons the Gila Bend bank's money will end up in a safe in Diego's San Miguel *hacienda.* Courtesy of a Mex called Galeana, some kind of swashbucklin' bandit. Years ago, he tangled with both the Rurales, and the Texas Rangers.'

'A lot of breath left in that dying man.'

'Struggling to confess. Hangin' on for dear life.'

'So now we know the name of the bank robber? The man who hightailed for the border?'

'But only bits of the story. There's a lot of banks in

100

Arizona. When we get face to face with this Don Diego, he's going to tell us why, if he was so desperate to get his money back, he and Galeana chose the one in Gila Bend.'

PART TWO

PROLOGUE:
DEADLY HIATUS

'In just a few short days you have, to a certain extent, put right a wrong that has been darkening every day of my life for thirty years. The Mexican sun has shone, warmed my body with its heat, but always in my mind it has cast a long shadow. So, you have done well. I am in your debt.'

'Your praise is generous, but I was not one hundred per cent successful. I understand that what has been returned to you is less than was stolen. I should be thanking you for your understanding.'

'My understanding is that from a sum of money stolen over thirty years ago, I am lucky indeed to get any return.'

THE GALLOWS AT GILA BEND

'But can you forgive the thief, a man who has shown no remorse during all those long, empty years?'

'Once a thief, always a thief. Lavished on such men, forgiveness is a wasted sentiment. However, you are wrong about empty years: I have prospered; my family is rich. But, as I have said, the wrong has been righted, but only to a certain extent. There is unfinished business, and it is what comes next that is of interest to me now.'

The two men were talking in a large room shaded from the intense sun by thick velvet curtains. Most of the furniture was old, dark wood, the wooden floor polished to a high sheen. The older of the two men, known by all as Don Diego, was sitting in a high-backed chair at a dining table covered by a white cloth. With swept back white hair he was well into his eighties, tall and thin, his clothes and his skin loose on a body that was still strong, upright. From time to time he sipped deep red wine from a cut crystal glass. His dark eyes were unreadable. One hand stroked his neatly trimmed white goatee as he watched the man who, several days ago, had ridden south and west from the border with Arizona.

Santiago Galeana, lean and raw-boned, had the wolfish look of a Mexican bandit but was a former member of the Guardia Rural, the Mexican army's gendarmerie. Off duty one exceptionally hot night in Nuevo Laredo, he had objected to an innocent jest and left a corpse sprawled on the floor of a cantina in a pool of blood and mescal. He had fled before he could be dismissed from the force for violent conduct.

Eluding pursuit under the wan light of a lambent moon he had headed north, and over time had followed the smell of money to the Diego estate. There, he had been fortunate. On the day of his arrival, Don Diego had at last discovered, from an unnamed source, the whereabouts of a man who had robbed him of a large fortune, made his way to the Pacific coast, and vanished. To Don Diego, Galeana was simply another common man who had appeared from nowhere and would accept money to do an uncommon task.

And so it had proved. But now . . .

'This area of interest. . . .' Galeana said. 'If it is a part of what happened in Arizona, a continuation, shall we say, then perhaps I can again be of use to you.'

'The money has been returned to me,' Don Diego said. 'Now I want my son.'

'Ah.'

Galeana nodded thoughtfully. He was standing between the table and the window. With both hands he held his sombrero respectfully in front of him, without intention hiding the gunbelt with its worn six-gun and loops of shells, the knife at his left hip in a tooled leather sheath. It was of the knife that he was thinking as he formed the words in his mind, though, in truth, the shape of the words could not be altered to blunt their impact.

'Don Diego,' he said, 'it is with sadness that I must tell you your son is dead.'

In the dark eyes, there was no reaction.

'Dead, how?' Diego said.

'The process of recovering money stolen from you

involved unavoidable violence. Your son was caught up in that violence. He died when his throat was cut by a killer without mercy.'

'The killer is known?'

'Oh yes.' Galeana said. 'He is a *gringo*, an Englishman with hair like straw, blue eyes with the look of ice. He has a reputation. It is said that he is a *mal hombre*.'

'Then I send one bad man to catch another,' Diego said, in that single slip of the tongue revealing his contempt for Galeana. 'I want you again to head north. This time, on your return, instead of money, bring me this *mal hombre*, this *gringo*.'

'I am honoured by your request,' Santiago Galeana said with a cruel smile, 'but I can decline it without any disrespect, and save you some money. It is my understanding that the *gringo* who murdered your son is already on his way here.'

'He has a name?'

'His name,' Galeana said, 'is Born Gallant.'

CHAPTER FOURTEEN

'I now know how those old-time pioneer families used to feel,' said Born Gallant. 'Wearily holdin' slack traces while tired horses, mules, pulled loaded Conestoga wagons across an endless sandy plain. Ridge of purple hills throwing long shadows, and always those Indian braves on the skyline, silhouetted against the setting sun with lances and whatnot. There at dusk, there at dawn. The stuff of nightmares.'

'Those fellers tracking us,' McCrae said, 'are Mexicans with modern weapons that kill from afar.'

'And this is Mexico, so there's no shortage of reinforcements, should our swaggering demeanour prove intimidating.'

'It's me that's intimidated. I counted three out there. Been with us since the night we came over the border. Big sombreros. Big show of crossed bandoliers, brass cartridges shining in the sun. Christ, I'll swear they're laughing at us, convinced I can see the flash of white teeth in swarthy faces when they grin. There may be more of them, but if it's just those three we're already outnumbered, outgunned.'

'But in no danger. You said tracking, I say escorting.'

McCrae looked questioningly across at him. He was riding off to Gallant's left. He and his horse looked, Gallant thought, like life-size sculptures created from grey clay by Remington, then coated in red dust for realism. Two days in desert country without respite, arroyos that were bone-dry watercourses. Tepid water in their canteens for drinking, not washing. For them, and the horses. And Gallant knew that his own valiant roan was suffering.

'I say escorting,' he said, 'because I don't for one minute believe the unknown Mexican who made off with the bank takings is stupid. He doesn't know for sure his two countrymen died at the Martins' house. Heroes are the stuff of myths; he has to believe they talked to save their miserable skins when they were taken behind the jail and got an eyeful of that wooden gallows.'

'If he's smart enough to work that out, he's smart enough to know the Gila Bend law will do nothing.'

'Yes, but, thanks to your journalistic outpourings and Gila Bend mutterings, my inflated reputation will warn him he's not yet out of the woods.'

'Then he'll have sent those bandits out to stop us well short of San Miguel. Gallant, do you suppose that escort's out there to make damn sure we ride into a prepared ambush? We ride into the next arroyo and fail to emerge?'

'Supposition is dangerous, Stick. An ambush is just one possibility. Supposition could also lead us into believing those fellers out there are riding for pleasure, and that ride happens to be taking us all in the same direction. Nonsense, wouldn't you say? So instead of supposin', why don't we get tricky, put 'em to the test?'

After a moment's thought McCrae said, 'Sure, why not? Turn around, point our mounts' heads towards Arizona, make 'em believe we're running scared, riding like hell for the safety of home territory.'

Gallant grinned. 'Just like our dearest Melody, you never let me down. But there's no rush. A simple homeward-bound canter will be enough to shock them into action.'

It was a landscape where distant horizons were lost in shimmering heat haze, scattered with low scrub, a stony desert with slabbed earth baking in the late morning sun, the rise and fall of its wide-spaced contours measurable only against the height of the lofty saguaro. As Gallant and McCrae turned their horses and put them to a gentle trot in a north-easterly direction – the sun at their backs – they knew that the Mexicans they were testing were on the other side of one of those low ridges that masqueraded as high ground. The direction they took would carry them past the point were that ridge petered out. Even if the Mexicans were not constantly on the lookout, at that moment the sun would pinpoint the two riders the way a spotlight might pick out the chorus line's star dancers.

They were spotted much sooner. They'd gone no

more than half a mile when, from unseen gunmen behind that ridge, three spaced shots rang out. Moments later, seemingly appearing out of the thin, hot air – the clusters of tall saguaro had many uses – another half mile ahead of Gallant and McCrae three riders deliberately made themselves visible. Broad sombreros, ragged ponies, again the glint of brass cartridges – but added to that hint of menace the sunlight flashing on metal barrels as rifles were flourished on high.

'The odds just doubled,' McCrae murmured.

'In their favour, and I was wrong,' Gallant said, reining in, again turning the tired roan. 'Those fellers behind the ridge are not an escort. They're shepherds, we're the sheep, and they've just set the dogs snapping at our heels.'

'Setting to one side your picturesque imaginings, nothing's changed but the timing,' McCrae said.

'Yes. But that delay was necessary, and revealin': they're shepherding us to a place where they think the killing will be easy. Maybe allow us liquid refreshment in the cantina, knowing that drink fermented from cactus juice turns the best of men into clowns. But they're living in dreamland. If we can reach San Miguel with the sun well down, in the shadows of narrow streets winding between adobe dwellings, these two wise gringos will give 'em a hard run for their money.'

CHAPTER FIFTEEN

As they approached San Miguel in the darkness of a moonless night it was clear to Gallant that the idea of losing themselves in narrow streets winding between shabby adobe dwellings had been fanciful, and wrong. And he quickly realized that his foolish optimism had been fuelled by memories of Salvation Creek, its single narrow street winding uphill from the Last Chance saloon, houses and streets like jagged lines drawn by a child with a blunt pencil. Places to hide at every turn – though hiding had not been an option when on the run with an angry Melody Lake cracking the whip.

San Miguel, in sharp contrast, was a Mexican pueblo built on flat land, without form, without shape. In England, Gallant thought, it would have been a hamlet with pretty houses clustered around a village green where the central pond was a reed-fringed splashdown for colourful ducks. But San Miguel was bone dry. There was no greenery, and the single-storey flaking adobe houses had been built where the head of exhausted incoming families had said, flatly, '*Aqui*,'

110

and had drawn wagons pulled by lathered mules to a final, creaking halt.

Several lifetimes ago.

If the San Miguel that had arisen stone by stone from the desert sand had a focal point, it was the cantina, the place where hard men drank hard liquor to drown sorrows. And this late at night – gone midnight, by Gallant's reckoning – it was the only building with light spilling from small windows. That weak light painted the walls of those adobe dwellings lying closest to it a dull yellow, drew blurred reflections from dusty windows. Low-slung houses fifty yards or more further away appeared as grey, misshapen boulders in the dark, their unlit windows like black holes where birds of prey nested and sharpened hooked beaks.

'Those gun-toting shepherds have been quiet,' McCrae said after a while. 'They were always there, making sure we saw them now and then, heard them in the hours of darkness – but now we don't.'

He and Gallant had drawn their mounts to a halt in a shallow dip in the trail. Saddle leather creaked when they reached into saddlebags for water canteens. Bridle metal tinkled when Gallant's roan tossed its head. It walked sideways, legs crossing, tail swishing, nudged McCrae's mount. And somehow, these natural movements in the unnatural stillness increased the tension.

'Their job's done,' Gallant said of the Mexicans who had formed their menacing escort. 'The ambush didn't happen, was never intended. If there is to be a killing – unlikely, I'd say – here's where it will happen.

111

But when they make that try, it will be at a place of my choosing.'

'Yours?'

'This is where we split up.'

'Too risky, Gallant.'

'No, it's common sense. If we both die, nothing's been achieved.'

'Which is not entirely surprising,' McCrae said, 'seeing as I, for one, have no idea what we're supposed to be doing.'

Gallant grinned in the darkness. 'No more do I, old son, so now I do some poking with a blunt stick and see what transpires.'

'Where?'

'The one place where people are awake.'

'And while you're doing that, where will I be?'

'Lying low,' Gallant said. 'Listening for the start of furious affray, the sound of breaking glass, then getting there fast to save an unworthy life.' He paused, thought for a moment. 'D'you still do that coyote call?'

'Sure. It startles folk, raises embarrassed laughs around late night campfires.'

'But now it needs to do something more serious. If I'm out in the open surrounded by Mexican bandits wearin' evil grins, I'll need reassurance, something rousing to bolster sinking spirits. The nearby throaty cough of a coyote. . . .'

'You're crazy.' McCrae swore softly, but without malice. 'Walking into that cantina, Gallant, could be as close as a man can get to committing suicide, short of cutting his own throat.'

'I've a feeling that getting out of that hot little cantina with skin intact will be the easy bit. It's what comes next, out in the wide open spaces of a Mexican night, knife-wielding bandits lurking behind each one of those lofty saguaros. Or should that be saguaro, singular and plural, one and the same?' He grinned. 'But talk of knives will always remind me of what I saw in the bank, what we both saw in the bedroom at Martin's house. Gruesome images that stick in the memory. They could make a brave man's blood run cold when faced by unshaven men wearing big hats.' He grimaced. 'Don't ask me why, Stick, but what happened – or didn't happen – when we'd crossed the border into Mexico tells me that I'm wanted alive. When I stroll into that cantina, pale of face, the only gringo in town, there'll be a glass of that Mexican poison waiting on the bar and. . . .'

A pause.

'Go on,' McCrae said. 'And?'

'And,' Gallant said, his eyes suddenly distant and cold, 'the man buying that drink, waiting for me with some kind of a proposition, will be the feller with the bloodstained knife who rode away from Gila Bend with his saddlebags stuffed with stolen cash.'

CHAPTER SIXTEEN

When Gallant brought his roan out of the dark into that yellow pool of light there was just the one pony at the drooping hitch rail fashioned from twisted mesquite poles. Which signified very little. Most peons would live close enough to the cantina to walk there, toss back green mescal from a succession of greasy shot glasses, then stagger home. If one man made his way there on horseback that would, perhaps, suggest a certain elevated status – even if, Gallant noted as he swung down from the roan, the horse that the man owned was in a worse state than the rail to which it was tied.

Which, again, could mean everything, or nothing – could even be a cool bluff to deceive the unwary: my horse is nothing, therefore I am a nobody.

And that's me thinking nonsensical thoughts to delay the inevitable, Gallant admitted with a rueful grin. Yet there was surely nothing nonsensical in memories of a razor-sharp knife sticky with blood, of dead men with gunshot wounds and blind eyes, or of the

114

knife's Mexican owner who had contrived to have Gallant and McCrae shepherded to the small pueblo of San Miguel.

Or so Gallant believed.

Or was that another figment of his imagination? Were those armed shepherds merely simple goatherds laughing as they passed the time playing harmless games with gullible gringos?

It was time to get to the truth.

Gallant flipped back his flat-brimmed black hat so that it hung between his shoulders, ran fingers through his long fair hair to make damn sure it didn't go unnoticed, then used his booted foot to kick open the door to the cantina.

His entrance impressed nobody.

Well, why would it? Strong liquor dulls the hearing, and while the light from smoking oil lamps might leak out of the cantina to paint nearby stucco walls, in that single narrow room it was fighting a losing battle against smoke that curled around worm-eaten wooden rafters and hung in flat clouds beneath the ridged shingle roof.

Smoke from the oil lamps themselves, sharp enough to bring tears to unaccustomed eyes. Smoke from the glowing tips of several thin cigarillos, for there was indeed more than one man standing at the bar. Gallant's entrance hadn't caused a stir, but it had not gone unnoticed. Men with drooping moustaches and liquid dark eyes shadowed by the brim of the inevitable Mexican sombrero had turned their heads to observe the newcomer. Eyes darkly luminous but devoid of emotion had taken in the mop of straw hair, the black attire grey with desert dust, the Colt Peacemaker in its holster tied low on the tall man's lean right thigh.

Then, with barely concealed contempt they had turned back to their shot glasses, their strong tobacco. There was a brief mumble of words spoken in Spanish too fast to follow, but which brought a sly grin from the fat, sweating bartender. And Gallant was forced to admit that this deliberately insulting behaviour was more than justified, for what use would his single handgun be against men who, even while drinking, did not divest themselves of the heavy crossed bandoliers of glinting brass cartridges that carried the same warning here in San Miguel that he and McCrae had heeded on the long trail from Arizona.

Not simple goatherds, then.

And that description would never fit the man who sat at the single table in the centre of the room. Relaxed in his chair, he was leaning back, lean, rangy, armed with a heavy, worn six-gun that Gallant knew instinctively would always rank a lowly second to the knife in a tooled leather sheath at his left hip.

In a smoky room that was no different from tribal drinking dens Gallant had walked into in the hills of Afghanistan, he was once again feeling the menace of hard characters armed to their stained teeth, and one who was clearly their warlord. Which, in Gallant's opinion, could be handled in only one way. In for a penny, in for a pound – and without allowing time for hesitation, he went straight to the bar and thrust himself between two of the drinkers. His wrist brushed

116

against a sheathed knife. There was movement along the bar as the pushed man lurched sideways. Cartridges clinked in loose cross-belts. A head turned Gallant's way. As the sombrero's drooping brim brushed his ear, narrowed dark eyes squinted at him. Reeking of cigar smoke, stale sweat, and enough garlic to make a man's eyes water, the man sneered, then grudgingly gave Gallant space.

'Thanks, old chap,' Gallant said. Elbows planted, he caught the bartender's eye and jerked his head towards the seated man.

'Has he got a name?'

For a moment there was a hush. It's as if I'm in a church, not a cantina, Gallant thought, and someone's just uttered a nasty swear word. Trying not to smile, he watched and waited.

'Galeana,' the barman said at last, for some reason keeping his voice down to a hoarse whisper. 'That man is Santiago Galeana.'

'Well,' Gallant said, 'Señor Galeana looks as if he could do with a strong drink. Let me have two glasses of that cactus juice that's turning these gentlemen cross-eyed.'

The barman's moist face twitched. His black eyes flickered, from Gallant to Galeana, and back again. Then, with a hand scarred by a knife wound, he swept a large cracked jug from a shelf, slopped liquid with a chartreuse tint into two shot glasses and slid them carelessly to Gallant.

'Awfully good of you,' Gallant said, gingerly dipping the tip of a finger in the spilled liquor. 'I believe Señor

117

Galeana has recently come into a considerable sum of money. He's a rich man, so make sure he doesn't walk out without paying.'

Deliberately adopting the ease and assuredness of a man confident of his own ability to face any situation, Gallant crossed the room and sat down at Galeana's table. He put the drinks down, met the lean man's gaze squarely, and shook his head in feigned disbelief.

'You play strange games, here in Mexico.'

'Games?'

'You know what I'm talking about.'

'What I know is you are talking tough, to impress, but it is still nothing more than talk.' Santiago Galeana had almost black eyes with as much expression as wet rocks in a cold river. 'Providing an armed escort for two men crossing a strange land is not a game. It is evidence of my concern for their safety.'

'Your concern, or Don Diego's?'

'Ah. You are well informed. But perhaps his concerns become my concerns.'

'I was informed by a dying man, who found the breath to hint at your reputation,' Gallant said, and watched for a reaction from Galeana that didn't materialize. 'All this concern for my safety, I wonder why I don't feel honoured?' He picked up his glass, tasted the strong spirit, then grinned at the lean Mexican. 'This Diego feller, you work for him?'

'When certain services are required, I am always available.'

'Bandit work? Like the recovery of stolen money? So why did it take you so long? Law officers giving you a hard time? I hear it's been thirty years.'

'Stolen thirty years,' Galeana said contemptuously, 'but for me it was just six months to find, and recover.'

'No. You robbed the Gila Bend bank, old chap. That money is not Don Diego's.'

'Oh yes,' Galeana said softly, 'it most assuredly is his.'

'Well, damn me, d'you mind explainin' how you work that out?'

'If I tell you that it was his son who robbed him, all those years ago, does that help?'

'In another time, another place maybe. But here it's late at night, and the old brain's a bit numb. Also, I'm sitting in a smoky cantina surrounded by armed men drinking strong liquor, and I'm faced by a man who admits he robbed the bank in Gila Bend. And by so doin', admits to a number of brutal murders.'

'Surrounded?'

'Figure of speech, but relevant nonetheless. Those men at the bar, they're all listenin', Galeana – the silence is deathly; hell, they're even taking care swallowin' so they can hear what's bein' said. They're waitin' for your signal. A snap of the fingers. A swift glance.' Gallant paused. 'When that comes, I'm a dead man.'

'But no. No finger snapping, no sharp-eyed glance, for surely it would be wrong to kill a hero?'

'There, I must admit,' Gallant said, 'you've lost me.'

'It is another reason for the escort, the shepherding across the plains when you and your friend crossed the border. Don Diego wants to meet you, because he believes you saved his son's life.'

'The son who ran off with a fortune. . . .'

'But who, nevertheless, is still his son and heir.'

'Problem is, Gila Bend will remember me, not as a hero, but as the damn fool who allowed a kid to be hanged. And worse. I couldn't save the life of a dog.'

'But when you are taken, now, to meet Don Diego, you will listen carefully, and everything will become clear.'

And now there was a sharp snap of the fingers. Movement at the bar. Gallant felt his back prickle, the muscles tighten instinctively in anticipation of the bullet, the sharp blade between the ribs. Then there was the scrape of boots on a dirt floor, warm tainted air moving against his face – garlic, sweat – and the man Gallant had elbowed aside was now at his shoulder. Short, muscular, a man strong enough and wicked enough to deal out death without compunction, without resorting to a knife or the crossed ammunition belts and the scarred rifle that had appeared from nowhere.

How many more of those peons, Gallant wondered, had similar weapons propped up against the bar?

'Pepe will ride with you to Don Diego's hacienda,' Galeana said.

'And our unfinished business? Me makin' damn sure you pay for bank robbery and murder?'

Galeana grinned.

'If you return, I will always be here.'

'And live, or die, to regret it,' Gallant said.

But as he walked out of that smoky hell-hole of a

cantina, it was the 'if' in Galeana's last words that caused Gallant to frown uneasily. He'd been promised a hero's welcome at the hacienda. Could it be that Don Diego had other ideas, all of them bad?

CHAPTER SEVENTEEN

There was no sign of Stick McCrae.

The Mexican climbed aboard the ragged pony and, without waiting for Gallant, rode away from the cantina in a roughly north-westerly direction. Heavy in the saddle. Legs flapping. One hand on his sombrero.

Better ahead of me than behind, Gallant judged. He mounted the patient roan and set off at a brisk canter in pursuit of his escort, figuring that at least he couldn't be shot in the back. And at once cast that optimistic notion aside, because hadn't he already wondered at the number of weapons available to the men standing at the bar? Looked at in that light, if one or more of them emerged, and followed, then the trap would have snapped shut.

Is that what Santiago Galeana had meant when he said 'If you return'? And if Galeana had as good as confessed to the bloody killings in Gila Bend, why was he still sprawled in a chair, smoking and drinking with a sneer on his lean face and his black eyes glittering? Why, in the name of God, hadn't Gallant settled the matter there and then?

Curiosity, that was why – and sadly, he knew damned well what curiosity did to the cat.

A hasty look back assured him that it was so far, so good – light spilling only from the cantina's windows, none from the door which he had pulled to behind him. And no sign of riders.

The trail snaked across a terrain with more ups than downs, the whole wild, dun-coloured landscape lit by a high moon unhindered by cloud. It was the point in any twenty-four hour cycle when the heat of the Mexican day was at its lowest, which for Gallant made it the most comfortable. On that slight but unending upward gradient he eased the roan forwards so that he was crowding the pony and Pepe, the Mexican rider heavily encumbered by arms and ammunition. Rode that way for a quarter hour, but got no sense that the Mexican was in any way troubled.

Why not?

Five minutes later another swift look back gave Gallant the answer. His roan and the pony had been kicking up dust, which was taking time to settle. Through it Gallant could see four riders. The dust haze turned them into phantom riders, ghostly shapes, yes, but clearly identified by moonlight glinting on metal bridle links and brass cartridges in crossed belts. Innocent shepherds, showing their true colours. A quarter mile back. Spread out in a wide line, well spaced.

And then Gallant and his guide rounded a high bluff, an unusual rocky outcrop in that mostly flat region. The moon shone brightly on the bluff's scarred northern face, against which clustered a veritable forest of saguaros. Impossibly tall and green, arms outstretched displaying countless sharp spines.

Some way ahead, not more than half a mile away, a house sprawled across a wide plateau like a discarded block of pure white alabaster.

Don Diego's hacienda, Gallant thought, with a sudden sense of foreboding.

And then, somewhere behind the nearby saguaros, a coyote howled weakly, coughed, and was silent.

'*Buenos noches, amigo,*' the Mexican said, and without suspicion, laughed hoarsely.

'And *hasta la vista,*' Gallant added, softly, fervently hoping that the coyote calling plaintively out of the darkness was the two-legged kind with worn boots, inky fingers and the intelligence to know that Gallant was in deep trouble.

Hock deep in the mire, Gallant thought grimly; and for an instant he considered spurring ahead, belting the lead Mexican across the back of the head with his trusty Peacemaker and joining the wily coyote in the maze of lofty cacti. But that would be leaping from one prickly situation into another much worse, he thought, grinning; death by a thousand painful scratches.

With a quick glance back down the trail, he settled to meet and tackle whatever lay ahead.

Before half of that last mile had been ridden, the four following Mexicans had closed up and positioned

124

themselves two on each side of Gallant. Not close in, but their mere presence – the creak of saddle leather, the clink of weapons and shells, the occasional smothered rasp of hoarse laughter – was a threat difficult to ignore.

But ignoring it became easier than Gallant had anticipated. The hacienda they were swiftly approaching was an imposing sight, made more so by Gallant's memory of the dirt-poor cantina and adobe dwellings of San Miguel. The eerie light of the moon that hid its inevitable decay gave this rich man's dwelling a touch of grandeur.

The roofs of Don Diego's hacienda were terracotta tiled. The main building, of white stucco, had two storeys. All windows – mostly tall, slender and arched – were guarded by iron bars embedded in the stone. From each end of that main building, single-storey wings extended at right angles, forming a courtyard that was enclosed on its open side by a low wall capped by more terracotta. At the centre of that wall, high and arched, a gilded iron gate shone with the glint of pure gold.

Not a single window showed any light.

The gilded gate was closed.

And the lead Mexican, Pepe, had turned his horse and was now taking his ragged pony along the wall. The escorting Mexicans split up. Two faded away into the darkness, their job done. The remaining two positioned themselves behind and to one side of Gallant as Pepe rounded the wall and headed for more low buildings that formed their own enclosure behind the hacienda.

Stables, Gallant surmised.

But surely stables, reeking of horses and ordure, were a strange place for a man of Don Diego's wealth and position to welcome a hero?

Like a much smaller version of the hacienda, the low-slung, flat-roofed stables were arranged in the shape of a three-sided square. Here, the open side was not guarded by a wall, and Pepe rode straight in on to earth hard-packed by the trampling of countless hoofs, and swung down from the saddle. He appeared to be waiting.

Gallant followed suit. The two men who had been riding behind him closed in, dismounted, and began crowding Gallant. He grinned at their greasy, moustachioed faces, the blank black eyes; noted the way their rifles, the woodwork bleached by the sun and worn smooth by rough hands, were held with the care a man might lavish on a beautiful woman.

Or on a dog, Gallant thought, that has been trained to sink sharp teeth into an enemy's throat.

He turned away, stretched lazily, made a play of easing stiff muscles, and used the action to mask a swift glance at his surroundings.

The horses were stabled in the two wings. He could hear the soft sound of their movements, a breathy snorting. The building equivalent to the hacienda's main house appeared to be empty, disused. Until tonight. Until a man called Born Gallant had walked into a Mexican cantina and allowed a killer named Santiago Galeana to talk him into a trap.

Maybe. But he still had his weapons. The

126

Peacemaker. A knife tucked away in his right boot, which could be useful, Gallant thought. Bandits were not heroes, and who could say how a Mexican would react when his throat was the one feeling the caress of cold steel?

Then, sharp on the still night air, there was a hard ring of iron on iron. Pepe turned. Away to his right, in deep shadow cast by the light of the moon, a heavy metal bolt had been worked, a double door had opened wide. Suddenly the sound of the resting horses became clearer as a man emerged from the stables. He stepped out of the shadows into cold moonlight. Tall, lean, dressed entirely in black, he held himself regally upright, the moonlight touching swept-back white hair, glinting on the high cheekbones of a face made to appear longer by the trim white goatee. The eyes were lost in dark sockets beneath the prominent brows.

He kept walking, hands behind his back; elegantly, without haste. Directly in front of Gallant, he stopped. And now the eyes were visible. Black, Gallant saw. Like the clothing; like, he guessed, the bitter thoughts that were compressing the man's lips into a thin line and causing those black eyes to flash with the fire of barely suppressed anger.

This, surely, was not a man who would consider a stable yard a fitting place to welcome the man who had saved his son's life.

Pepe put his rifle's butt on the dirt, let the weapon rest vertically against his hip. Then he doffed his ragged sombrero and with both hands held it to his chest. Gallant took note of that pose, saw how it kept

127

both those hands occupied.

Behind Gallant there was a whisper of sound as one of the Mexicans mumbled under his breath *Hail Mary, Mother of God*, spoken in his native tongue. In that instant Gallant felt his blood run cold, knew that the old man in black had chosen this location for an execution.

'It is, I would suggest, a suitable occasion for prayer,' said the old man. The thin lips smiled at Gallant, but the black eyes remained cold, merciless. 'Perhaps you have a favourite you would now like to say, standing, or on your knees in the dirt, as you choose – in the few moments you have left on this earth.'

From behind his back he brought a heavy pistol, and cocked the hammer.

Pepe moved to one side. Boots scraped on the hard earth behind Gallant as the two Mexicans drew apart.

Getting out of the line of fire, Gallant thought. Can't say I blame 'em. But they're in no danger. This old boy's got a steady hand, and he's standing close enough to drill the centre out of the ace of spades.

Very softly Gallant said, 'I don't have much time for religion, or faith in prayer, Diego.'

And as if in resignation, his eyes lifted to the flat roof of the building behind the man in black. The night sky, made luminous by the moon. And seen against it, in silhouette. . . ?

'Did my son pray. . . .' Don Diego said, '. . . before you cut his throat and left him to bleed?'

'If I knew his name. . .'

'His name is my name.'

'Diego?'

'Martinez.'

Gallant shook his head. 'Mexicans died in Gila Bend, but I never did know their names. Two I killed – but not with a knife. Those, and the white man and woman who had their throats cut, died at the hands of another Mexican. We both know his name. The man and the woman he murdered owned the bank. *Their* names. . .'

Gallant stopped. And then he rocked back on his heels, shook his head, as in that instant most of what had happened in Gila Bend began to make sense.

Don Diego Martinez was watching him with contempt. The levelled pistol had never wavered. The man's knuckles gleamed white on the grip, the trigger.

'Names mean nothing. You are a worm wriggling on the hook, Gallant, but in your heart you know that a hook has barbs and the worm is always doomed. . .'

While talking he had been lifting the weapon. He brought his other hand from behind his back, used it to steady the heavy pistol. Gallant found himself looking into the yawning blackness of the muzzle. In that moonlit moment it seemed that the world was holding its breath. He realized again that he had not been disarmed. His Colt Peacemaker was in its holster – which, for all its usefulness, could have been in the next pueblo, the next Mexican province. Don Diego's bullet would hit him before his own palm slapped the Peacemaker's grip. And yet, what choice did he have. When faced with certain death. . . .

'Stop right there, Martinez, get your finger off that

trigger. I'm up above you, drawing a bead on the back of your skull. I'm a crack shot with a rifle. Gallant dies, you die. Your choice.'

The clear voice rang out in the still air. It made nonsense of veiled threats and circumlocutions with a blunt warning that could not be misunderstood.

Diego Martinez looked at Gallant. And now there was a tremor in the levelled pistol. A thin, crooked smile moved the thin lips, but it failed to mask the man's uncertainty, his indecision.

'She said it,' Gallant said, 'and you'd better believe she means every word.' Without waiting for Diego's response he stepped forwards and plucked the pistol from the stunned man's limp grip, threw it far away behind him.

'Is Stick up there with you, Melody?'

'In the trees, fifty yards behind you. Military tactics. We set up a cross-fire.'

'Damn me, but I've got you well trained.'

'Then you should know that what comes next is a tactical retreat, with covering fire. Mount up, Gallant, and get the hell out of there.'

CHAPTER EIGHTEEN

Martinez had not moved. The man's old hands, already turned bone white by the fierceness of his grip on the pistol, were now tightly clenched. Gallant, the man Diego Martinez would have put to death, had left him standing there and was away and running. He reached his roan by roughly brushing aside Pepe and the other Mexicans. As if turned to stone, they fell back stiffly as Gallant's weight hit them, but made no move to prevent his escape: it seemed that all of them were watching Diego Martinez, waiting for a word of command.

None was forthcoming. An old man's brain was refusing to work. Gallant was being gifted with precious time.

He reached the waiting horse, threw himself bodily into the saddle and kicked hard with his heels. The roan reared once, forelegs thrashing, then dropped down and within four long, raking strides was into a full, eager gallop.

Gallant took the horse straight for the open side of

the square. Once through he squinted ahead and used knee and reins to make the slight change of direction that saw him heading for the stand of stunted, parched pines mentioned by Melody Lake. It was close, no more than fifty yards away.

He had covered half that distance across the sand and wiry grass when from those trees a dazzling muzzle flash was followed by the crack of a shot. A bullet hissed through the air close to Gallant's head. Then ahead of him a horse burst from dark shadows into bright moonlight, its rider standing in the stirrups, waving a rifle.

'They're after her, Gallant,' Stick McCrae yelled. 'Three of 'em have run for that building. They'll be through and out the back doors before she can drop from the roof and reach her horse.'

He was still yelling when he settled in the saddle, stretched forward along the horse's neck and raced past Gallant. Ignoring reins, gripping with his knees, McCrae rammed the rifle butt into his shoulder and fired another two shots.

In the open square where Diego Martinez stood without movement, a man cried out in agony. Gallant, wheeling the roan to follow McCrae, saw one of the running Mexicans fall. The other two disappeared from sight as they kicked open a door and entered the building.

Then Gallant had brought the faster roan alongside McCrae.

'Look, Stick,' he gasped. 'Look, up there. . . .'

Melody Lake was not fool enough to be caught cold.

132

She had heard Don Diego at last unfreeze and snap an order; had seen the Mexicans look up at her, then run for the building. Now she was up on her feet, a slim figure with a rifle, outlined against the night skies. Calculating that she could not leave the roof at the rear of the building and get to her horse before the Mexicans burst from the back door, she made what was, for her, a logical decision: if she couldn't go back, go forwards.

'She'll drop down into the square,' Gallant said breathlessly, holding the galloping roan alongside McCrae. 'You go for Diego. Stop him from reacting. Smack him on the head, kill him if that's what it takes.'

'And you?'

'An aristocratic gentleman,' Gallant said, grinning, 'always has time for the weaker sex.'

Moving apart they raced into the square. McCrae rode fast for Martinez, dragged his horse to a halt and tumbled from the saddle. Then Gallant left him to it. His whole attention was focused on the flat roof. He took the roan in at a fast curve, brought it alongside the low building's stucco wall.

Melody Lake was standing at the roof's edge.

'Gallant, take hold of this,' she cried, and tossed her rifle into space.

He caught it left-handed, passed it to his right hand and, with the reins bunched, held the roan steady. Without hesitating, Lake dropped flat on the roof, slid over the edge and let herself down until she was hanging by her fingertips. Then, with one backward glance, she kicked herself away from the wall. Gallant

133

held his left arm crooked at the elbow. Lake grabbed it. Clung on. Her weight threatened to drag Gallant from his horse. She touched the ground only lightly. Then she was up again. Kicking her leg over the roan, she straddled the horse behind the saddle and wrapped both arms around Gallant's waist.

Her face was turned so that her cheek rested against his back.

She was shaking with laughter.

'Damn fool,' Gallant said shakily.

'Get us out of here, Gallant.'

'Here, take this.' He passed back her rifle, felt a hand grasp it. 'What about your horse?'

'Just move. You'll see.'

The Mexican McCrae had shot was still down. There was no sign of the other two. McCrae had rendered Diego harmless by forcing him to his knees in the dirt, then holding his pistol against the old man's head while he watched Gallant and Melody Lake. Now he holstered the gun. He shoved Diego flat on his face, then swung into the saddle, rode after Gallant and drew alongside the galloping roan.

'Once out, head north,' Lake said.

'It's not over,' Gallant said. 'Martinez thinks I killed his son. He won't let it rest.'

'Then we ride fast and hard,' McCrae said. 'We've seen half-a-dozen Mexicans, but there'll be many more – too many.'

But they both knew Melody Lake wasn't listening.

As they rode away from the square Gallant felt her tense, then let go with the one arm that was still

keeping her secure. She took a deep breath and whis-
tled, loud and shrill, close enough to Gallant's ear to
make him wince. Seconds later he heard the fast
pounding of an approaching horse's hoofs. Away to his
left a pony came racing from behind the stable block,
loose reins flying, stirrups flapping.

Again the whistle, this time more muted.

The running pony swerved, galloped straight for the
roan, came alongside.

And suddenly the warmth of the young woman's
body had left Gallant's back. With the lithe skill of an
Indian brave Melody Lake had leaned far out.
Somehow still clinging hold of her rifle, she'd reached
for her pony's saddle horn and vaulted from one horse
to the other. Then, with a merry whoop of joy, she
spurred away from Gallant and McCrae and within
seconds had gained twenty yards, then thirty.

'Follow me,' she cried, 'if you're good enough. And
you need to be. If you look behind you you'll see that
most of Don Diego's peons are up on horseback, and
riding like the wind.'

CHAPTER NINETEEN

Melody Lake's estimation of the number of Mexicans in pursuit was a wild exaggeration driven by her hot-blooded excitement.

This Gallant established by constantly glancing over his shoulder as, obeying her clarion call, he sent the roan racing up the wide moonlit trail in the cloud of dust raised by the feisty young woman and Stick McCrae.

So, not *most* of Diego's *peons*, but certainly enough of them to be a damned nuisance. Half-a-dozen, say? And, as Gallant's frequent glances soon told him, their movements suggested that knowledge of the area would give them an advantage.

He touched the roan lightly with his heels. A more powerful horse than those ridden by Lake or McCrae, its long strides ate up the ground and it brought Gallant alongside the pair without noticeable effort.

'Where are we going?'

'Arizona, in one hell of a hurry,' Melody Lake said, rolling her eyes as she looked at him as if talking to a rather slow child. 'But first we make a brief stop at woods where I spent the night, pick up my bed roll. . . .'

'The trail bends to the west before straightening and arrowing north for the border – is that right?'

'Clever of you to work that out. It's already doing so, Gallant.'

'Ignorin' childish sarcasm, it seems Don Diego's poor peons are about to cut us off at the pass. They've left the trail. Straight line, shortest distance between two points and all that. . . .'

'It's only a couple of smelly blankets,' Stick McCrae said, grinning at Lake. 'Leave 'em for the peons. We can head north from here.'

'Blankets, plus papers in a briefcase that I took from my saddle bags and stuffed under a bush for safety.'

'My inclination would be to go with Stick's idea,' Gallant said, 'but if those papers are important. . . .' he saw Lake's firm nod '. . .then we'll go for the woods. But listen. . . .'

He slowed the roan, drew rein under a stand of saguaros in rough grass off the trail, waited in a pool of deep shadow for the others to gather round.

'We're outnumbered, but if we split up, lack of numbers becomes an advantage. Hit and run, don't you know. In and out, makin' them scared of their own shadows.'

'Any skirmish that follows won't last all that long,' McCrae said, nodding. 'They'll get ahead, wait for us. We follow the trail, eyes and ears open. Soon as we get sign, we split, come at them from three directions, and it'll be all over.'

'You two boys do love talking,' Melody Lake said caustically as she wheeled her horse and made as if to ride off.

'Wait.'

She turned to glare at Gallant.

'They don't know where you spent the night,' he said, 'so they're not going to be a row of fluffy ducks sitting by those woods waiting to be shot.'

'You mean they'll rejoin the trail, but they're not going to wait out in the open?' McCrae said.

Melody was nodding.

'No. If we can split up, so can they – and they will. It'll be a dose of our own medicine, a deadly crossfire from ambush. Your idea was a good one, Stick, but we're in desperate need of an alternative. Gallant. . . .'

But Gallant was no longer listening. He lifted a hand for silence, and in it they all heard the ominous rattle of hoofbeats.

'Damn it, we've got it entirely back to front and have spent too long talking,' Gallant said softly. 'The horsemen I saw leave the trail are already back on it, and returning. Those that never left are also makin' their move and coming up behind us. I reckon the next voice you hear could be your last – an excited Mexican, giving the order to open fire.'

They still had time. The curve in the trail meant that the Mexicans returning could be heard but not yet seen, while it was doubtful if those in sight and hammering up the back trail could see their prey.

By chance, Gallant backing off the trail into the

138

shadow of the saguaros had put the fugitives out of sight and gained them precious seconds.

'That ambush is ours to set up,' he snapped. 'You two, get behind these saguaros. I'll cross the trail, but make damn sure I'm seen. They see me, they'll think all three of us have gone that way. . . .'

Still talking, he was already on the move. He took the roan across at a leisurely trot, heard a wild cry from the horsemen approaching from two directions and kicked his mount into a faster pace as he left the trail. Looking around he saw rocks, rough scrub – but nothing to provide cover from flying hot lead, and mere seconds to get settled.

He dropped from the saddle, slipped his rifle from its leather boot and slapped the roan to send it safely away. Then he dropped prone behind a low rock. Sharp stones bit into his knees, his elbows. He wriggled for some relief, some steadiness, cocked the rifle.

Across the trail he could see the saguaros, but no sign of Lake or McCrae.

Then, in a thunder of hoofs and with a volley of wild cries, the Mexican horsemen came together. Horses circled, backed, snorted in the swirling dust. Rifles were waved with the keen shine of brandished swords. Sombreros dangling from plaited cords on sweat-soaked backs were splashes of colour in the moonlight. Once again Gallant noted the crossed ammunition belts, saw the glint of brass cartridges – was absently amused at such macho posturing.

And so he waited, and tensely wondered – but not for long. The time that passed was measured in seconds. He was not kept in suspense.

For their planned manoeuvre the Mexicans had split into two groups of three. Now, at a snapped command, the six of them turned as one and spurred their horses off the trail. Straight towards Gallant's position. Whooping it up, yelling to create fear: they were expecting three, not one man totally exposed.

Then, from the saguaros some way to their rear there came a loud, mocking hail:

'Over here, you damn fools, we're behind you.'

Consternation. Orchestrated by McCrae, Gallant knew full well. Neither journalist nor lawyer could bring themselves to shoot a man in the back. So the jeering call tried for two things: to give Gallant more precious seconds, and to bring the assailants face to face.

And so it was.

As if following a script written by Stick McCrae, the Mexicans jerked leather reins taut, brought their ponies to a ragged halt, and twisted in the saddle to look back for the unexpected threat. The rapid crackle of rifle fire from McCrae and Melody Lake was instant, and deadly. Two of the Mexicans pitched from the saddle. Sombreros were like colourful capes flapping. Their limp bodies bounced on the hard ground, and were still. The other four parted, milled, uncertain whether to continue towards Gallant, or go back over the trail to face the blistering fire from the rifles.

Again a snapped command. All four turned their backs on McCrae and Lake and charged Gallant's position.

Gallant brought one down with a snapped shot. Leaving three. Then he was thrown sideways as a bullet chipped the rock in front of him and a splinter of stone struck him on the temple. It was like being hit by a Mexican knife thrown with uncanny skill. Pain shot through his skull. He went down, momentarily seeing life through a red haze. And that life looked exceedingly short as one of the remaining Mexicans was down off his horse and leaping at Gallant with a drawn knife.

Play possum. Play dead. Old advice heard on the burning slopes of Afghanistan saw Gallant flop sideways and lie still, his eyes slitted. His vision cleared. The Mexican leaped the rock. More rifle fire crackled. An unseen Mexican cried out in agony. Two remained – but one of those was close, and intent on murder. Gallant caught the reek of stale sweat as the Mexican rammed the heel of a booted foot into his ribs, lifted the glittering knife high, held it poised for a second.

Then, even as the knife began its swift, deadly descent, the Mexican was jerked back with the suddenness of a running steer hitting the end of the cowboy's taut reata.

Dragged away, snarling his protests, by another Mexican.

And now, lying doggo but with everything in his line of sight sharply etched, Gallant saw who had saved him from death – or rather, he corrected, the man who had saved him only so that he could be the one to take Gallant's life.

'Didn't recognize you,' Gallant said, rolling on to his back, then sitting up. Warm blood was running down his face as far as his jaw. He swiped it with his hand, wiped his sticky hand on his pants. He grinned at the tall old man, got his feet under him and managed to stand shakily upright.

'After our previous interesting encounter,' Diego Martinez said, 'I find that difficult to believe.'

'Different chap altogether, don't you know. Borrowed sombrero, crossed cartridge belts over a jacket you must have stolen from an old nag ready for the knacker's yard. Damn it, Diego, I took you for one of those useless peasants.'

The insults passed over the *caballero*'s head. Once again he had the big iron pistol in his hand, pointed with great steadiness at Gallant.

'Can you think of one reason,' Diego Martinez said, 'why I should not pull the trigger and send you straight to Hell?'

'I can,' Melody Lake said, her voice piercingly sweet. 'If you want your son, then you need to ensure that Born Gallant stays alive.'

She and McCrae had ridden across the trail from the shelter of the saguaros. Down off her horse, Lake was holding her rifle, but not using it as a threat. It seemed, Gallant thought, that she was relying on her skill as a lawyer to save the day.

'My son is dead. Killed by this man.'

'No.' Lake shook her head. 'Dead, yes, but murdered by Santiago Galeana.'

Don Diego shrugged his shoulders with great elegance.

'Dead is dead, and even if Galeana was the dealer,

142

this man played a hand. . . .'

'Behind your hacienda,' Melody Lake said softly, 'you must have a plot of land you consider sacred. That will be the place where, over the years, you have buried your dead.'

For a long moment there was silence.

'What is it you are saying? Is it that. . . ?'

'Gallant, alive, will return to Gila Bend. He will have your dead son taken from the ground and placed in a fine casket with brass handles and a silken lining. He will ensure that he has the use of a black hearse – perhaps of the undertaker himself – and he will bring that casket across the border from Arizona so that you can inter your son in that sacred ground.'

'Why Gallant?' Martinez was attempting insouciance, but in his black eyes there was the wet gleam of emotion. 'What you are describing does not need this man – Gallant is not important, not necessary. Gallant dead simply means that someone else – you, perhaps, guiding the man with his hearse – can bring my son home.'

'No. Gallant has the authority. He was for a while the Gila Bend marshal, and is respected. He can order an exhumation. Only Gallant can arrange for your son to be brought home – and anyone looking at you now can't fail to see that you are desperate for that to happen.'

Diego tilted the big pistol away from Gallant, eased down the hammer.

'You are persuasive.'

'The decision is yours, Don Diego. If Gallant dies

here, now, you die with him. You will die without the satisfaction of knowing you have killed Born Gallant – death in an instant snatches awareness – and your son will spend eternity rotting in a cheap coffin in the Gila Bend cemetery.'

CHAPTER TWENTY

'Nothing else he could do,' Stick McCrae said. 'He wants his son's body, and he saw me as the danger, not the talkative young lady lawyer with her rifle. . . .'

'Now just a minute, McCrae. . . !'

'. . . because men of his race and kind know that women have their place, and that's in the home cooking meals and. . . .'

'. . . and being justifiably feared by men taken prisoner in wars whenever and wherever you care to mention.'

'Damn right,' Born Gallant said. 'Service in Afghanistan drills home that lesson pretty sharply, if that's not a tasteless way of puttin' it. But settin' all sick jesting to one side, tell me, Melody Lake, what brought you galloping into Mexico on your white steed to snatch me yet again from the jaws of death?'

'The men sitting in a Yuma office, who will be my partners in law. They have had dealings in Mexico with Don Diego Martinez, and with a certain person of dubious rectitude in Gila Bend.'

'But when I was bein' escorted to a place of death by those heartless Mexicans, you and Stick were working as a team. Care to explain?'

Melody grinned. 'Sheer good luck. All the way from Yuma I had this mental map of the hacienda's location. When I got there, the place was in darkness, but there was some movement in the stable yard. I caught a glimpse of one man, in shadow but his white hair shining, heard your name mentioned. Very concerned, I pushed on for San Miguel, and bumped into Stick.'

'And the rest, as they say, is history.'

It was halfway between midnight and dawn. Martinez had returned to his hacienda to organize the recovery of the dead Mexicans. He'd gone unwillingly, packing away the big pistol with obvious reluctance, and had done so only because he had seen, in Born Gallant, a man who would stick to his word: his son would be brought home in style.

Gallant, feeling his own earlier suspicions justified by Lake's news, was sitting with her and McCrae around a crackling camp fire. They were in the woods where Melody Lake had left what Stick McCrae had sarcastically described as a couple of smelly blankets, and a briefcase containing papers that she deemed important. The blankets, crumpled but clean, were folded. She was using them for a cushion. The briefcase, of worn, scarred leather, was by her side.

'Callin' someone a fellow of dubious rectitude is a sublime example of understatement in lawyer speak,' Gallant said, 'but it makes a lot of sense, and matches my thinkin' entirely. Discussed it with Stick before we

146

left, liked the sound of it. Someone in Gila Bend was smart enough – or lucky enough – to link bank owner John Martin with the Mexican thief, Juan Martinez. But for that to be of any financial use to them, they had to know the full story.'

'The Gila Bend man with a crooked bent has a legitimate sideline in horse breeding, but mating inferior stallions and mares led to poor quality offspring. Difficult to sell to knowledgeable Arizona ranchers, so Mexico looked attractive. A bit of digging came up with the news that a haughty *caballero*, name of Martinez, was always on the lookout for good stock.'

'A sideline,' Gallant said. 'Meaning this feller had other gainful employment.'

'But it wasn't making him rich, and future prospects were limited in a town the size of Gila Bend,' Melody said. 'So our horse breeder rode south of the border and quickly discovered that Don Diego Martinez liked to talk. He gave up the idea of peddling inferior stock – Martinez was having none of it – but became a willing listener for an old man who had never come to terms with past iniquities. Large sums of money were mentioned, and the seeds of murder and larceny took root in a greedy man's mind.'

'I'm beginnin' to think,' Gallant said, 'that the papers stuffed in that worn leather briefcase will add credence to the ideas bouncin' back and forth, turn fairytales into fact.'

'Damn right they will,' Melody said. 'Don Diego Martinez pulled a lot of Mexican wool over our failed horse breeder's eyes. He wanted to recover all or some

147

of the money stolen more than thirty years ago, and he
was good at listening as well as talking. That crafty old
Mexican went along with ideas he knew were criminal
and careless of human life – even named the man he
would pay to do the dirty work. . . .'

'Santiago Galeana.'

'Yes. Then he covered his back by talking to those
new lawyer pals of mine and telling them he'd done
the exact opposite.'

'All recorded in plain English?'

'In detail.' Melody Lake grinned at Gallant. 'Care to
take a guess at this horse-breeder's legitimate employment?'

Gallant hesitated.

'There's a gallows in Gila Bend,' he said softly. 'It was
intended for a young drifter who put a bullet in ex-
Ranger Bill Owen, and we know what happened to
him. But after he was strung up from a tree overlookin'
Boot Hill, things got much worse, the killings more
bloody. Can I take a stab at a name? Well, lookin' at
Stick nodding tells me we've reached the same conclusion. Melody, the name your lawyer pals have written
down, the man behind all that thievery and bloodshed,
has to be a Gila Bend town councillor. And the only
one we know is my pal Ed Logan.'

CHAPTER
TWENTY-ONE

Gallant rode into Gila Bend with Stick McCrae, but without the lovely Melody Lake. Sick and tired of galloping from all points of the compass to save Gallant's life – Gallant was grinning when he suggested this to McCrae – she had ridden directly north from the camp fire in the woods, heading for Yuma and oak-panelled offices where lawyers might trade insults, but rarely bullets.

The ride in a more easterly direction took Gallant and McCrae a day and a half, which saw them ride into the town of Gila Bend in mid-afternoon. There they put into action the plan they had discussed on the long, hot ride. Gallant rode straight up the bustling main street, knowing full well that a man in dusty black attire with his flat black hat doing little to cover straw-coloured hair would attract instant attention. McCrae cut up one of the narrow alleys between business premises, intending to work his way around the houses and come into town from the east.

They would converge on the jail and council offices. Timing had not been discussed. McCrae swore that he'd be in place when needed, but unobserved. Gallant was deliberately announcing his presence in Gila Bend, and awaiting with interest Ed Logan's reaction.

As always, events took a turn for the worse.

At an angle to his right across the street Gallant saw, through the dust raised by horses and wagons, a tall man leave the jail. Mexican clothing, but no crossed gunbelts. Sombrero at his back. He unhitched his horse, led it to raucous curses and shouts of protest through the hubbub of a working day, and stopped outside the council offices. There he ignored the hitch rail, instead ground-hitching his horse by leaving the reins trailing. Then he took a canvas-wrapped package from a saddlebag, and went into the building.

Gallant heard the faint bang as the door was slammed.

Santiago Galeana.

Well now. Back in San Miguel he had called Gallant a hero, then sent that hero to Don Diego Martinez, having signed his death warrant. It was logical to assume Galeana believed Born Gallant dead: a man alone, escorted by a bunch of armed Mexicans, had been delivered to a dignified caballero with revenge in his heart and his lean, veined hands holding a gun.

So, in the belief that he had got rid of Gallant, the rampaging knight errant, Santiago Galeana had ridden to Gila Bend with unfinished business. His entering the council offices confirmed what Gallant and McCrae had worked out and what they assumed Melody Lake's lawyer partners had put in writing: that Ed Logan was the man behind the Gila Bend bank robbery, and the wrapped bundle being delivered by Galeana had to be Logan's share of the spoils. Banknotes, stained with blood.

But what of the new town marshal, Don Makin? Why had Galeana called at the jail first before conducting his business with Logan? Had there been two canvas-wrapped packages? Was Makin in league with Logan and Galeana?

Letting his horse move easily with the flow of the mid-afternoon bustle, Gallant drew rein and dismounted outside the council offices, hitched the roan alongside Galeana's fine mare and glanced up the street.

Stick McCrae was approaching, unhurried but observant. With a flick of his hand no higher than hip level he made it known that he was watching Gallant.

Then another door banged as Don Makin, badge glinting in the sunlight, came out of the jail office and started across the street.

Planned, normal daily routine – or because he'd seen Gallant arrive?

Keeping his right hand free for the Colt Peacemaker, Gallant used his left hand to open the office door. He strode into comparative gloom, smelling like every remembered school room but also reeking of stale cigar smoke.

Tables, filing cabinets. Leaflets and calendars

pinned to walls. A couple of the new typewriting machines. Against the wall an iron stove, cold on this hot day. Three men.

Earl Sedge, the tall leader of the town council, was standing behind one of the tables. His hunter's face, with the eagle nose, the sharp eyes, was grim. Ed Logan was at the end of the table. The canvas-wrapped package lay on the table. His jacket, Gallant noticed, was pushed back from the butt of his six-gun.

Close to Logan, Santiago Galeana reacted to Gallant's arrival with the speed of a striking rattlesnake. Before the sound of the door opening had died away, Gallant found himself covered by Galeana's heavy old six-gun.

'A dead man walking,' Galeana said softly.

'That must be it,' Gallant said amiably. 'That, or old age must be takin' its toll. Beaten to the draw by a minor Mexican bandit,' he marvelled. 'Damn me, but that's a bitter pill to swallow.'

'What the hell's going on?' Earl Sedge said. And to the braced, armed and dangerous Galeana, 'And who the hell are you?'

'Allow me, Sedge,' Gallant said. 'The feller's a Mexican bandit, name of Galeana. The man responsible for the recent bank robbery and most of the murders.'

'If true,' Ed Logan said in the voice of authority, thrusting out his chest, flicking a glance at his superior officer, 'then I was absolutely right in my judgement and you have to be congratulated, Gallant.'

'You're jumpin' the gun, Ed,' Gallant said.

'Responsible for the bloodshed, yes, but Galeana wasn't the man hopping back and forth across the border doin' all the organizing.'

'Of course not. One only has to look at the man. No doubt he's a hired gun, paid by someone high up in his home country, a crooked man with a high opinion. . . .'

'Well, you'd know all about that. Don Diego Martinez, the man you played like a fish. His son owned the bank, and died there.' A pause, to let the words ring, be absorbed and understood by Sedge. Then, 'Care to tell us what's in that canvas bundle?'

'I have no damn idea. That man burst in here when Sedge and I were talking business, slapped this package on the table. . . .'

He was cut off by the opening of the street door. Marshal Don Makin walked in. As he stepped inside, Santiago Galeana spun, fired a wild shot at the marshal, took two fast steps and dived headfirst through the window. The window's wooden frame splintered, was carried out on Galeana's shoulders. Shattered glass rained down on the street, sparkling in the bright sunshine.

In the raw stink of spent cordite Makin stumbled back against the door. Galeana's bullet had nicked his left shoulder. Blood blossomed, spread, seeped down towards the shiny marshal's badge. Makin's face turned white. He reached up instinctively to clap a hand to the wound, then checked the move and went for his gun.

As the crunch and tinkle of shattered glass and timber died away there was a burst of six-gun fire from the street. Someone hollered, a roar of anger. A

153

woman screamed. Then there was a rattle of hoofs. A horse snorted, another shot cracked.

Stick McCrae, Gallant thought, and grinned. But his blue eyes were cold with the realization that while McCrae could use the whole street in a fight to the death with Galeana, in the council office there were too many men, too little room.

But was there really anything to fear from the out-numbered Ed Logan?

Well, a rat in a trap and all that, Gallant thought—

And Logan made his move. Taking advantage of the distraction outside, he snatched up the canvas package and struck wildly backhand. Earl Sedge ducked, but took a heavy blow to the side of the neck. Off balance, he staggered away from the table. Still holding tight to the package, Logan went for his gun.

Gallant was between door and shattered window, facing Logan. As the councillor made his draw, Gallant flapped a hand at the wounded marshal – stay out of it – and leaped for the near end of the table. He drew as he ducked beneath the heavy wood. Logan's shot cut a deep groove in the table's top, thumped into the far wall. His second chipped a splinter of wood from the table leg closest to Gallant: the councillor had also ducked down, and fired at Gallant from under the table.

Behind Gallant, Don Makin ignored the signal to lie low. He sprang away from the door. Using his weak-ened left hand he gripped the table top in the centre of its long side. With a mighty heave with hand and hip that brought a groan of pain from between clenched

154

teeth, he tipped it over. It hit the unsteady Sedge and he was again knocked backwards. He wobbled on unsteady legs, fell against the cold iron stove. The tipped table settled, lay rock steady on its long side.

Born Gallant and Ed Logan were exposed. Two kneeling men facing each other with drawn guns aimed and cocked.

Gallant was the first to react.

He laughed.

For an instant the totally unexpected bark of mirth seemed to freeze Logan. Then he brought his left hand over and rapidly fanned the hammer of his six-gun. Three shots rang out. The bullets hammered into the far wall. The intended target had moved. Gallant had followed the deliberate, distracting laugh with a sideways dive. It took him around the fallen table's top. Again he was under cover.

But his desperate dive saw him crack his wrist against the heavy timber and his Colt Peacemaker flew from his hand, slid across the dirt floor.

Unarmed, he flashed a glance at Makin. But the marshal was down. His move with the table had sapped his strength, and he was losing too much blood. Ed Logan was up on his feet, coming around the table. His face was drawn, anguished – a man in torment. By Gallant's calculation, the councillor's six-gun held four empty cartridges. Two bullets remained. Just one of them would finish Gallant.

But Logan, with eyes only for Gallant, had forgotten Sedge. The last blow he had taken had knocked Sedge against the stove. From its stone base he had snatched a heavy fire iron. As Logan came round the table, Sedge gripped the iron with both hands. He swung the makeshift weapon in a wide arc, with all his strength. The heavy metal struck Logan's right arm just below the shoulder. There was the sickening crack of breaking bone.

Ed Logan moaned, shut his eyes and dropped to his knees. The six-gun, with its two remaining bullets, dropped from nerveless fingers.

Sedge, still holding the fire iron, looked over at Don Makin. The marshal was out, unconscious, his blood soaking the dirt floor. Sedge turned to Gallant.

'You were the marshal. You know the office, the layout. Take this apology for a man, and throw him in a cell. In the morning – dawn's the best time, or so I've been told – in the morning, make damn sure he's taken behind the jail and hanged by the neck until well and truly dead.'

EPILOGUE

Santiago Galeana had made it out of town. Ground hitching his horse in front of the council offices had been done with an eye to possible flight. With fragments of glass glinting on his shirt he had leaped into the saddle and made his break towards the western edge of Gila Bend. He managed to do that down the crowded street by riding along the plank walk. The scream heard in the council offices came from the woman Galeana's racing horse knocked through a shop window.

Stick McCrae had been taken by surprise. Caught fifty yards away towards the wrong end of town, he had been prevented by the crowds of working townsfolk from taking a shot at the fleeing bandit. Instead, he had fired into the air, but that had been a feeble reaction gaining him nothing. The crowds milled. They blocked the street and the plank walk. McCrae was left to watch Santiago Garcia bring his mount nimbly down off the plank walk, turn to give a mocking wave, and ride out of town.

Nobody died on the Gila Band gallows.

When Marshal Dan Makin regained bleary consciousness in Doc Olson's surgery he was able to enlighten Gallant on the reason for Santiago Galeana's brief call at the jail. The Mexican had wanted to know where he could find a certain Gila Bend councillor – a man by the name of Earl Sedge.

Gallant's mistake – and Melody Lake's before him – had been in not reading the papers stuffed in the young lawyer's briefcase. Had they done so, they would have seen that the man who was full-time councillor and part-time horse breeder was not Ed Logan, but Earl Sedge.

And Earl Sedge had vanished, along with the canvas-wrapped package that had lain on the table. Between the two councillors, yes, but always intended for Sedge. Acting like a guilty man, Ed Logan had fought simply because any man will when he can see his remaining life on earth measured in the hours to a cold, hanging dawn.

Two days after the fight in the council offices, Stick McCrae left town to take up his employment with the newspaper in Yuma.

And just another week later, Born Gallant again headed for the Mexican border. He was driving the Gila Bend hearse pulled by the undertaker's noble chestnut mare, undertaker Eli Gaunt having declined the invitation to accompany him. His roan was trotting behind at the end of a rope. In the glassed rear interior

158

of the hearse the exhumed body of John Martin lay in the silken lining of an expensive timber coffin with brass handles – paid for by a certain English nobleman.

Born Gallant was keeping his word.

Whistling somewhat off key, his mind always fondly with Stick McCrae and Melody Lake, he was taking Juan Martinez, the thief who had used money stolen from his father to found the Gila Bend bank, back home to Mexico.